The Boy with the Golden Horn

A Tale of Waddyshire

Doris Gaines Rapp

The Boy with the Golden Horn
A Tale of Waddyshire

Doris Gaines Rapp

Daniel's House Publishing
Huntington, Indiana

Copyright 2022 Doris Gaines Rapp
Huntington, Indiana 46750

website: www.dorisgainesrapp.com
contact: dorisgainesrapp@gmail.com
blog:　　www.tuckermcbrideintheclassroom.com
Subscribe to my weekly newsletter, News from Tucker McBride's World
https://lp.constantcontactpages.com/su/mAwV0CW.

Cover design is a drawing by the author, Doris Gaines Rapp, and put in place by @Debi Lindhorst/The Type Galley.
Chapter heading artwork of deer by MugiMulya/Shutterstock.com

Library of Congress Control Number: 2022905441

ISBN-13: 978-1-7365110-5-3 (paperback)
ISBN-13: 978-1-7365110-6-0 (eBook)

~ 5 ~

Dedication

Dedicated to all those who want to be somebody
and don't realize they already are.

Acknowledgments

A big thank you to my writing friends. Your presence and positive encouragement are blessings to me. Thank you for sharing your faith in God.

Thank you, Vicki Borgman, for your willingness to read, *The Boy with the Golden Horn* and give feedback.

Debi Lindhorst of The Type Galley in Warren, Indiana, you can do all the computer stuff I can't. Thank goodness you're gifted in geek.

I also thank others who willingly read pre-publication copies of *The Boy with the Golden Horn*. You find what I never even see, yet know it is there.

Table of Contents

Chapter
                                                              Page

Chapter One

A Treasure Found

"Jackson, Jackson Jones," a voice whispered from the far side of the window, like a breeze rustling the heather.

Jackson threw back the coarse spun sheet his ma had woven and peered out his loft window. Who had called his name? He scanned the heathland that stretched beyond the village to meet the forest. He could see violet flowers blowing gently in the moonlight. But no one was there.

When fifteen-year-old Jackson finally got up that morning, in the spring of 1846, he had no idea how fast his life would change. "Come, boy," he called to his dog.

Months before, the Shaman-fey hiked into the high hills above the village of Waddyshire and set up camp. From up there, he brought nightly terror to the villagers.

No one could understand. A Shaman is supposed to be a messenger between two worlds, the human and the spiritual, for good or evil. The Shaman-fey chose the evil forces from the unholy world to achieve his own wicked motives. But Jackson had no idea what those motives were.

"But today is peaceful and full of the promise of a good day, Dutch." Jack reached down and scratched the collie lovingly on the head. "The sun is warming the morning already. It should be warm enough to leave our winter coats behind. Let's go for a walk," he said to the Dutchman.

Before leaving the cottage, Jackson wrapped two pieces of honey-covered, thick homemade biscuits into a tattered white napkin. He stuffed the sandwich into the knapsack he carried over his shoulder. Also in the sack were two sugar cookies his sister Jemima whipped up and a pewter cup Pa made at his forge. Jackson knew where a fresh, clear stream ran through the forest.

Jackson and Dutch headed toward the forest above the village. "Look, boy," he said to the dog. "The sun has melted the frost from the top of the stone walls." The stacked rocks surrounding many houses kept the sheep in the meadow. Jack looked to the grasses stretching between the thatched roof homes and the common land. In their thick winter coats, the white woolies generously ate of the grass that had sprouted again after the last freeze. It was a beautiful day. High above the village to the east, Broadmoor Castle glistened in the light. The Earl and Countess of Moorland usually avoided the cobblestone streets of Waddyshire. They did their shopping, business, and socializing in Lochlan. A skylark started singing his song of the heath as he swooped along the top of the coarse grasses and violet blooms. The scalelike leaves of the small flowers formed low-growing mounds or spreading mats. The leaflets had tiny hairs, which gave the foliage a grayish cast.

Finally, Jackson and Dutch entered the wooded acres. Earthy-smelling green moss and purple wildflowers were beginning to cover the forest floor. "Ah," Jack said as he inhaled slowly with satisfaction. Again, Jackson wondered who had called to him during the night, but he quickly dismissed it.

Jackson had gone into the forest to hunt branches in the dampness of the deep woods. When he brought the small limbs home, he would lay the twigs out to dry in the sun before his mother used them as kindling for the fireplace. In the evening, Jack would switch out the wood he had already dried for the wet pieces and fill the wicker basket beside the fire with burnable tinder.

While in the woods, he would sit on the bench his great-grandfather made, rest beside the brook, and eat his breakfast. He enjoyed the job of foraging for small pieces of wood. Twice a week, it allowed him the time to wander through the forest for hours.

That morning, everything was the same, and yet all was different. Velvety green plants clung to the logs across Crystal Creek and created a rustic footbridge for forest walkers. As Jackson started across the bridge, he held the nearly-full basket of kindling above the water while peering into the creek below. Then something caught his eye. Perhaps it was a gnarled, artfully twisted branch sticking out of the creek bank. As Jackson looked into the shallow water at some smooth round rocks and the crazy-formed twig, his foot slipped on the slick moss. He fell in with a giggle and a splash. The warm day made the dunking a delightful late-spring experience. Jackson sat in the waist-deep water as Dutch joined him, romping merrily, and licking Jackson's face. Then the boy saw something quite unusual.

His father's grandfather built a large log bench many years before. The poplar-wood seat waited at the water's edge. The armrests were logs split the long way, forming a flat place to lean his arms, and more long split logs created the seat. The bench had been there so long that the wood had weathered to a rugged, slick patina. As Jackson sat in the water for a moment, he could see beneath the heavy, multi-person seat. Wedged up under the logs, in a tangle of thickets, Jackson spied a loosely tied draw-string bag with a shiny gold thing sticking out of the opening. The shiny metal object was bell-shaped on one end and had a mouthpiece on the other.

Quickly, Jackson climbed out of the water and tugged gently on the dusty pouch, not wanting to tear the old bag. It was easy to see the horn inside when he pulled the leather sack out. It seemed impossible to believe it could be under an old woodland bench. Once the bag was free, Jackson took out the horn and held it up to the late morning sunlight that streamed through the high canopy of branches. Jackson knew that his friend Rebecca Hampton's horn was brass, like the other horns musicians played in the village band. But for sure, the one he just found was different. It was twice as heavy as Becky's horn. Since Becky's and the other musicians' horns were made of brass, Jack knew this horn was definitely not brass.

Chapter Two

Digger Jinx

Jackson couldn't contain his excitement. His long legs carried him out of the forest and down across the heathland with Dutch at his heels. Jackson continued to hold the basket of large twigs in his left hand.

"Dutch!" Jack called to his collie. "Leave the weasel alone," he cautioned when a critter popped his head out of a burrow as the boy and dog darted past. "The bunnies too," Jack added as several small rabbits scurried back and forth, crisscrossing in front of them. A nightjar bird and two Dartford warblers flew to the sky, twittering about all the fuss. Jackson and Dutch kept going with a whop and a holler. Back in the village, Jackson jumped and twisted with joy as he ran along the cobblestone road to his house.

As he neared his home, he saw someone in the yard. Then, he remembered. Pa had hired Digger Jinx, the gravedigger at the Waddyshire Church cemetery, to replace some thatch blown off in the wind the night before. Most people in Waddyshire lived long lives, and Digger only received payment when he dug a fresh grave. Digger always needed extra work.

Jackson cringed when he saw the man. Most people in the village didn't trust Digger. The children were afraid of him. His smile revealed some missing teeth, and those that remained were yellow. Jinx found semi-fitting clothes in the mission box, cast-off ragged shirts and pants others donated to the church for the poor. Pa agreed to pay Digger for the thatch work. Digger would also get his shovel repaired at Pa's forge and a piece of Ma's apple pie.

"Where ya running to, Jackie Boy?" Billy Busby shouted from his yard where he worked grooming his horse. "Get that mount of yours ready for the big race at Craggy Crook Downs."

"Don't you worry about Champion and me, Billy." Jackson didn't stop but breezed on past his friend and rival. "Besides, the race is weeks anyway. And it's you who should be worrying." Jack couldn't wait for the big race. Maybe if he won, people would finally notice him. Now, he felt invisible.

Billy motioned to the ratty little man at the foot of the Jones' family ladder. "I see Digger is working for your pa, Jackie. How come Mr. Jones allows the likes of that man to step one foot on your property? Digger is a thief and scoundrel."

"That is Pa's business, not yours," Jackson spoke sharply. He didn't trust Digger Jinx either. But more than that, he didn't like Billy's bossy ways. As Jack hurried on, one thought continued to gnaw at him. *There is something about Digger Jinx that chills me.*

Chapter Three

The Mysterious Horn

As Jackson opened the wooden gate in his family's stone fence, chickens roaming in the large side yard flapped their wings and scattered away. His pa's blacksmith shop sat behind the thatched roof cottage. The boy grabbed the latch on the barn-style door to his father's forge and flung it open.

"Pa!" he called into the large shed that housed the forge his father had built years before. "Pa!" Jackson rushed in with the horn held high. He plopped the twig-filled wicker basket on his father's workbench and danced around the room. It had been so long since Jackson had something to celebrate and smile about, his face hurt. His father watched and laughed over at the bellows in front of the open stone fireplace. Jackson nearly stumbled over Dutch as the dog dodged between the boy's legs.

Dutch found a safe spot, once inside the forge shed, away from the boy's dancing feet and the flash of the fire. The collie kept his eyes on the anvil where possible chips might fly and lay down. He curled up on the floor and pulled his paws under his body to make himself as small a tripping hazard as possible.

"Jack," Oliver Jones gasped as the hammer slipped from his hand and created a ding in the buggy spring he was making. The spring would replace the broken one on Doctor Davis' carriage. "Stop your bouncing around. I still have Digger's shovel to fix."

"Sorry, Pa," Jackson gulped. "I'll help you fix it."

"Yes, I would appreciate that," Oliver sighed deeply. "That's your job for now. Have you thought any more about your work? It would be fine to learn more about the smithing trade. But you're a smart young man, Jackson."

"It costs a lot of money to go to University, Pa." Jackson reminded him.

"You've finished your eight years of school, Son. You're a young man now."

"I know, Pa."

Then, Oliver stopped and looked carefully at what Jackson held. "What have you there, Son?"

"I found the horn in the forest, under Great-Grandpa's log bench." Jackson's excitement mounted again as he presented his find.

Oliver Jones shook his head slowly. "That's where it has been?" He smiled broadly but did not reach for the instrument.

"What do you mean, Pa?" Jackson stopped and stared with wide eyes. "You've seen this horn before?"

"My grandfather talked about a golden horn." Oliver finally reached out for the glistening trumpet. "May I hold it?" he asked as Jack handed it over.

"It belonged to Grandpa's father?" Jackson asked.

"Yes." Oliver turned it around and around, his eyes appearing to disbelieve what he was seeing. "A village story says the Shaman-fey invaded the mountain caves years ago. No one knows his age. He was here when Grandpa owned the horn. The Shaman-fey said the music affected him strangely. He hated Grandpa's music. He said it made his body creep and crawl."

"Why?" Jackson asked with wide-eyed innocence.

Oliver explained, "When evil meets beauty, love burns off all the hate. If there is only hate, the person withers and dissolves into nothingness. The creepy, crawly feeling warned the Shaman to mend his ways."

Jackson studied the horn as his father held it in the wood and coal-fired forge light. "It is heavy for brass, Pa."

"That's because it isn't brass, Jack," Oliver whispered. "You must tell no one, Son." He stopped and looked toward the open door. With his hand placed to the side of his mouth, he spoke softly. "Your horn is gold."

Chapter Four
The Real Thing

"Gold?" Jackson gasped. "I've never seen real gold before. Are you sure?"

"Hush," Oliver insisted with a gruff voice. "Yes, it is gold. I have seen the precious metal. A few people have asked me to repair their gold jewelry. It is priceless. You don't want someone to steal it. Tell anyone who asks, 'Pa developed a special polish that makes my horn shine like gold. But of course, it's not. No one owns gold except the King.'"

There was silence in the room for a moment, except for the crackling of the fire in the firebox. Finally, Jackson smiled sheepishly. "You want me to tell a lie? You would have disciplined me if I had told an untruth."

"I know, Jack. But, it's also wrong to bring danger into our home if someone tries to break in and steal the horn. Here," he paused and took a polish-treated rag from his workbench. "I don't want you to tell a lie." He rubbed the cloth over the horn, making it shine even brighter. "See, it is the truth. The polish I developed for your ma's windows does make the horn shine."

The sun had gone behind the clouds, and the room dimmed. Yet, the gold shone like someone lit a candle. Jack and Oliver gasped at the brilliance of the horn.

Jackson grinned and took the horn in his hands. "It is amazing…enchanted. If we take it to Lachlan when we go to the fair, we could sell it for the price of gold." His head hung low as he added, "I know we can use the money."

"Everyone can use more money, Jack," Oliver admitted as he wiped his hands on his smithy apron. "Then, they find more things they want, and soon their extra money is gone."

"Maybe I should keep the horn hidden until we get our neighbors' reaction to the music," Jack offered slowly.

"Maybe you shouldn't sell it for a while, Son."

"Where do you want me to put it for you, Pa?" Jackson caressed the horn as if he were cradling a new puppy.

"Me?" Oliver's eyes sparkled. "Jack, my grandfather lost the horn many years ago, or the Shaman-fey stole it." He patted Jackson on his shoulder. "You found the horn, Me-Lad." He gave his son a sideways hug. "The horn is rightfully yours. Perhaps it will let you blow music through it."

"Mine?" Jackson couldn't believe his ears. "But I can't play a horn." He looked at his father hopefully. "I don't know how to. Do you?"

"No, Jack. I never put it to my lips." Oliver squared his shoulders and smiled. "The horn chooses the musician, not the player the horn," Oliver chuckled and raised his eyebrows. "The proof of your ability to make music will happen when you put it to your lips. If the horn lets you play, you are the rightful owner."

Jackson couldn't see how that was possible, a golden horn that chooses its own player. To his mind, that was silly; but his father didn't usually tell fanciful stories. Dutch raised on his front paws as the boy put the horn to his lips and puckered. The dog's ears flicked and waited. The melody reverberated off the wide-board shiplap installed on the northeast wall to cut the wind. This side of heaven's sweetest tones filled the forge, sending mellow sounds into every corner of the chinked log structure.

"The villagers will know you now, Jack." His father placed his hammer on the anvil and inhaled the beauty of the melody.

Jackson shrugged and whispered, "But if I'm not to let people know about the horn, they wouldn't know who is blowing it."

"With music like that coming from your horn, it doesn't seem fair they wouldn't know your name." Oliver agreed.

"They didn't know me before I found the horn," Jackson moaned into the mouthpiece, changing the timbre of the melody from joyous to plaintive.

"No, Jack," Oliver gripped his chest in pain. "Stop, please. The sad, angry music is killing me." He fell to the floor in pain.

"Pa!" Jackson choked on the notes. He started to put the horn down. Something terrible was happening to his father.

"No...don't stop. Play the sweet notes," Oliver begged as his breath grew shorter.

Jackson put the horn to his lips again and thought of the love his father had always shown him. He saw summer days at the fishing hole where the two of them laughed and threw their lines into the water. Later, Ma fried their fish for supper. Tears rolled down the boy's cheeks as he remembered a long winter afternoon with his father.

His father's pain subsided as the loving images flooded his memory and rang out through the horn's bell. Oliver struggled off the floor and climbed onto the old wicker chair sitting beside Dutch.

"Jack," Oliver wiped beads of sweat from his brow, "I forgot the other side of the magic in the horn. Even though it has a dark side, I will trust you to play the right music that will benefit your friends in the village."

Jackson thought for a minute. He smiled a little but admitted to himself, he had no friends in the village. Well, maybe a few. There was Rebecca and Billy, and perhaps more if he shared his friendship with them.

"Jack, listen carefully," Oliver stepped closer and whispered raspily. "Jackson, if you are sad, your music will moan, too. If you are angry, your melodies will send sharp blades of hatred into the listener's heart. But if you have loving memories, your songs will uplift the souls of those who hear them and bring joy to their lives." He stood up and put his hand on his son's shoulder. "I will not take the horn from you, Jack. The horn chose you."

Chapter Five

View from the Sky

That evening, Jackson grabbed the basket from beside the fireplace and took it out to the forge. His mum was ready to start supper and needed a good fire in the hearth. Jackson gathered the kindling he had dried during the day and headed back to the house.

"Good evening, Mr. Jinx," Jackson called as he dashed toward his cottage door. He tried to get past the janky man as quickly as possible. *Unreliable* at work was not a word to describe Digger Jinx. He was, however, every other word people used when they whispered about him. Maybe Jackson was wrong.

"Good day to you, young Jones," Digger Jinx said as he stopped measuring and cutting a thatch runner. As he started up the ladder, he asked, "What ya got there?" He pointed to Jackson's leather pouch.

"Hi, Mr. Jinx." Emma, a four-year-old, waved her first two fingers at the gravedigger and smiled as she walked on past.

"Hi, Emma," Digger said as he stopped and waved at the little one. She was in a little gray dress and white pinafore.

"You seem comfortable around little girls," Jackson said, studying the dingy man.

Digger's lame smile revealed his mouth full of gummy, blueberry-stained teeth. "She's a sweet little thing, isn't she? I appreciated her help finding Mrs. Farley's silver cream pitcher the other day."

Jackson tried to keep the conversation short. "She found it under the stack of thatch you had at the ready to repair Mrs. Farley's roof. You let the child get too close." Jackson stopped and studied the grizzly man for a few seconds. "I think Pa would appreciate it if you would keep your eyes on the roof repair."

Digger ignored Jackson and called after the child as she started for home. "Emma, wait." Jinx stepped down from the third rung of the tall wooden ladder stretching up to the roof's ridge peak.

"Wait?" Jack was surprised. How did Digger Jinx know any of the children in the village? "Her ma wants her at home." Ordinarily, parents kept their young children away from Jinx. Most of the mums and pops didn't trust Digger.

"Better hurry home, Emma." Jackson shooed the child off. "Your ma will be looking for you."

"Sleep tight," Digger called after her. "Dream up the place the Vicar's candlestick got to."

"The candlestick is in my pa's forge, Digger. The bottom has to be welded back on." Jackson was always suspicious of the man and even more so when he saw something shiny in Digger's lunch pack." Jackson had wondered why things often came up missing when the man was around. "What do you have there in your pack, Mr. Jinx?"

"Yes, Jackson," Digger smiled with a squint and a wink. "That's the pocket watch me father gave me." Digger folded his long, frighteningly sharp razor knife. Jinx slipped it into the leather sheath that hung from his rope belt.

Jackson stiffened and jumped back a step when he saw the blade.

Digger dropped the large, comb-shaped Leggett on top of a stack of water-reed thatch runners and grabbed up his lunch pack. The sharp hand tool was a regular part of roof repair, used to smooth out the thatch plug.

Jinx reached in the sack and gently pulled out a shiny pocket watch. After blowing his hot breath on the surface of the engraved silver, he rubbed the timepiece on his shirt. Then, he turned the timer over to reveal the lettering, *Jinx*, engraved on the back. Looking with pride at the clock's case, Jinx whispered, "This was me granddad's, and then me dad's."

"That's a corker," Jackson said as he admired the timepiece. "How did…? I mean, where—?"

Digger wiped the silver case on his dirty shirt again. "Where did me granddad get the money for this fine watch?"

"Well," Jackson stammered, "yes. That is a thought." Jackson looked away, embarrassed by his own question, and stumbled on a raised stone in the street.

"Me granddad was a watchmaker, not a sailor. He was working in his watch shop one day when a couple of blokes came in for watch repair. After Granddad finished the work, the fella didn't want to pay. An argument started that led to a fight. Granddad didn't know, but they were members of a press-gang. They kidnapped me grandfather and impressed him into the navy during a war in the early 1800s. Granddad smuggled his watch out before they set sail to give me father. He died at sea and never got back home. With Granddad gone, me father had to quit school as a young lad to support his ma and younger brothers and sisters. They had to sell their comfortable home to pay their debts. When the money from selling the house was gone, Grandma spent time in debtors' prison."

"Oh," was all Jackson could respond. *Who and what was Digger Jinx? That business about his grandfather explains how his family fell so far into poverty.* Jackson guessed he really didn't know Digger Jinx at all. "Well, you better get back to work," was all he could say.

Digger hoisted a stack of thatch runners to his shoulder and started up the tall ladder. "That's good." Halfway up, Jinx stopped. "I can already see all over the village from here." He looked east and west. "On the edge of the village, I see the Garver boy bringing in the family cow for the night. And, over on Lippincott Lane, Little Mary is gathering in her kittens before the shadows hide them."

Jackson smiled and snapped his fingers. *So that's how he keeps track of all the village children. He sees them from the rooftops all around the neighborhood.* Turning from Digger, Jackson added, "The wind has started blowing from the mountains in recent evenings. You probably have a lot of roofs to mend."

"You are right. A lot of thatch blew onto the heath." At the peak of the house, Digger dropped the thatch runner and let it unroll down the side of the roof. "Looks like I'll have extra work for a while. Little time to work on me water reed dolls."

"Dolls, Digger?" Jackson turned with his hand on the door latch. "Do you play with dolls?"

"No," Jinx started to laugh. "I sell them at the fair in Lochlan."

"You do?" Jackson scratched his head with the end of his horn pouch. "I didn't know you went to the fair. We go to the fair, too. I've never seen you there."

"The fair covers many blocks, Jackson," Digger said and smiled. "Your booth is close to other stores people shop in."

"How did you know that, Digger?" Jackson felt creepy, like eyes watched him from all directions.

"I've seen you there, Jackie boy." The old man, crinkled with embedded thatch dust, spit out some bits of reed. "I wash up and put on me granddad's tweed jacket."

"Oh, so you look different than this." Jackson looked at Jinx up and down. "That explains it." He lifted the front door latch, looked back at Digger, and shuddered. Stepping inside, he stumbled again. *Jinx,* he thought, *that's a good name for you. You are certainly a person who brings bad luck.*

~ 28 ~

Chapter Six

The Angry Wind

The upside-down weather had recently flummoxed everyone in Waddyshire. It was summer in southern Arie, but the evening hours chilled everyone down to their wool-lined slippers. A wind blew down from the hills in Teacup County. The average temperature at that time of year was around seventy degrees. Still, the icy wind lowered the temperature by twenty degrees. It seemed to continue to drop a little more, late in the evening, after the sunset. The villagers were frightened.

"Have you heard the horn player at night?" People in the village began to ask among themselves. "The music is so calming," they would say. But Jackson was quiet about everything: the horn, the music, and the one who played it.

"Jackson," Becky called after him one day as he pushed a wheelbarrow full of paving-stones he was to deliver to Vicar Turner. Large, smooth rocks lay at the mountain's base, tumbled, and shaped from rolling down from a higher elevation. The stones were there for the taking. The Vicar wanted to lay cobblestones at the front of the vicarage. He could sit there in the morning with a cup of tea and greet the villagers as they passed by on their way to school and neighborhood shops.

"Morning, Beck," Jackson responded. "Did you get your mum's garden weeded?"

"Every small blade and leaf," the girl said triumphantly. "Jackie, I got some news."

"News? In this little village?" Jackson kept the wheelbarrow going. It was much easier to hold the wheelbarrow upright if he kept it moving. Clucking, flapping chickens that had fluttered out of the neighbor's walled yard scattered as Jackson pushed his load along. Some feathers took to the air and bounced lightly on the breeze. "You'll have to walk faster, Becky. If this barrow falls over, I could up-dump the load here in the street. I want to surprise the Vicar by delivering these today, not tomorrow like he expects."

Becky hurried ahead, turned around, and walked backward. "I'm moving, Jackie. How slow do you think I am going? It looks to me like I'm ahead of you."

"Alright, you win." Jackson looked up toward the church and the residence beside it. He kept on pushing.

Becky waved her arms in excitement. "Simon Baker, the greengrocer, said his brother, George, had walked in from the lowlands. His fancy buggy horses hadn't come back to the stable after he let them out to graze. So, George went looking for them. It was getting so dark he wasn't sure of his footing higher up the mountain. If the horses had entered the cracks and crevices near the peak, he wouldn't be able to see them. He only had the moon to light his way."

"Becky, George Baker had no business up there. Some say the Shaman-fey set up a memorial for his daughter in one of the shallow caves." Jackson shook his head. "I sure wouldn't want to run into the Shaman at night. He has aligned himself with an un-holy, other-world patron. Now, the Shaman knows only evil."

"If George sees him, Georgie wouldn't recognize him. No one has seen the Shaman-fey," Becky insisted.

"Maybe there isn't a Shaman-fey in the mountains or anywhere," Jackson said as he turned into the walking path to the vicarage.

"I know the Vicar tells us there is no Shaman-fey," Becky lowered her voice.

"No, Becky. Vicar Turner said there is no Shaman with more power than God." Jack stopped the wheelbarrow and began unloading the rocks.

As Becky bent to help transfer the cobblestones to a pile on the ground, she whispered, "George heard the Shaman talking to himself. The Shaman mumbled, 'They will learn. I will punish them.' Then the Shaman sat at the entrance to his cave and inhaled deeply. His eyes glowed with hate and fear. Maybe the Shaman was afraid of his own power and what he was about to do. The Shaman-fey blew icy air into the dark night with his lungs full of freezing anger and hate. With each breath, the wind that blew became stronger and colder."

Jackson stopped and rubbed his hands together. "I don't understand. How can that be? A Shaman is a healer, a prophet. They can talk to the spirit world and get a spirit to help heal others."

Becky spoke softly. "The Shaman who looms over our village is also a fey, a clairvoyant. He can read your mind." She glanced toward the front door just as the Vicar came out. "Shh."

"Why are you shushing Jackson, Rebecca?" the Vicar asked.

"Sorry, Vicar," Becky apologized. "Jackson wanted to get these rocks for your outdoor sitting space delivered tonight as a surprise. I guess I spoiled that."

"Jackson," the Vicar exclaimed as he threw his hands up, "you are a blessing! Thank you."

Jackson smiled and added, "If you need help putting the stones in place, Vicar, I'd be glad to help you tomorrow."

"And I will be most happy to pay you, Jackson," the Vicar said, then looked at the sky above the high hills. "The wind is beginning to blow again. The people will all start going inside. They're afraid, Jackson. They don't understand the change in the weather. The cold wind could stymie the growth of the crops in the fields and the cabbage in the gardens."

"Maybe the horn player will blow those sweet, calming tones again tonight," Becky said as she wrapped her arms around her waist. "The music seems to make me less afraid."

The Vicar looked again at the hills. "We've all heard the hornblower. Who do people say he is who plays those happy melodies?"

"I haven't heard anyone say." Jackson told the truth. No one had guessed who played the songs in the night.

"I'm going to hurry home," Becky said as she brushed back some blowing hair from her eyes. As she left, the wind blew the hem of her skirt up, which revealed the lace along the bottom of her bloomers. "Oh, my," Rebecca said, straightening her hem. She grabbed a handful of fabric on the side to hold it down. "Sorry, Vicar," she chuckled as she turned and hurried home.

"I'll see you tomorrow, Vicar. Bye, Becky," Jackson said as he ran down the stone road and darted into his house.

"I'm home," he called in the direction of his mum and pa's bedroom. It had been a long day of hard work for both his parents. They had gone to bed at sunset on the summer day. "I got the cobblestones delivered, and I'll help the Vicar lay them tomorrow."

"Good, Jack," his mother said from the bedroom. Jackson saw the light dim as his mum lowered the wick in the oil lamp.

Jackson climbed the ladder to the loft. On the left, a short hall led to Jemima's room. Jackson's room was on the other side. When his little brother, Henry, was alive, the two boys shared the space.

Jackson reached up above the open beam of the first rafter beside the wall. Concealed in the space between the beam and the thatch of the roof, Jackson pulled out the valuable pouch. Quietly, he removed the precious horn, using the soft inside of the bag as a polishing cloth. With the latch to his window pulled down, Jack pushed it open. He blew the uplifting music toward the mountain from his window, allowing the hills to catch the melody and send it back to the village. The echo helped to hide the melody's origin. Jackson played the songs that calmed people's souls into the night.

Chapter Seven

The Deer

I know it may be hard to believe the word of an enormous sixteen-point deer, but Jackson Jones did. Jack remembered it all very well. It was magical that summer day in his father's field, where the sheep grazed on the evergreen shrubs of the meadowlands. The glossy, wavy leaves of the holly bush beckoned the holly blue butterflies to their sweet-smelling blossoms. However, the real miracle was the giant stag standing on a knoll at the forest's edge. The deer was talking to Jackson using perfect speech.

"Jackson, my boy. You are the one," the deer announced boldly, in deep, smooth-as-silk tones.

"What?" Jackson gasped, first at the thought of a talking deer and second at the words he spoke. "The one what?"

Jackson didn't believe he was special. He was born in 1831 when King Tapping was still on the throne of Arie.

Though Jackson had already lived fifteen years, he didn't think he had accomplished anything. School and helping his father in the blacksmith shop were the only accomplishments he could claim. To his thinking, gathering wood didn't count.

Yet, his neighbors and friends in Waddyshire thought Jackson Jones was the one with the talent. But they rarely told him. Jack could ride a horse at top speed and eat a whole gooseberry pie at the county fair faster than burly old Robert Fulton. Still, Jackson wasn't happy. He saw nothing special in the things he did.

None of my abilities are unusual, Jack thought. He didn't recognize anything he did as a talent. He thought everyone could paint a sunset and feel the warmth of the glow or compose a song of praise as soothing as one from David's harp. Jackson could. Most of all, it wasn't the *doing* that Jackson wanted to experience. It was the *being*. Jackson wanted acceptance by his friends and others in Waddyshire. If truth be told, everyone did believe in Jackson. Jack didn't believe in himself. He wrapped his arms around his belly as the sudden chill from the threatening wind blew even sharper.

Jackson was the oldest child in his family. When Jack was still in school, he was the only student in his schoolroom with an average mark in every subject. In a football match, the other players called him the stumble-king.

Besides his family, one creature showed him unconditional love, his eighty-pound collie dog, Dutch. The Dutchman was long-haired with a shiny sable-brown coat. Every evening Jackson would sit by the fireplace and comb Dutch's hairy coat to a silky sheen.

Jackson worked in his mum's garden early in the morning until lunch during the summer months. The sun was less vengeful at that time of day. Dutch would either stretch out in the shade as Jackson used the hoe or follow his boy up and down the rows of vegetables as Jack weeded. On the flatland, Jackson gathered grass for the horses.

The green vegetables had ripened in the garden that flanked the other side of the road. *Maybe the sudden chill won't damage the tomatoes and corn,* Jack hoped.

Jackson remembered the evening he first encountered the deer. After completing his chores, Jack had gone for a walk out into the fields. He had already brought the family's cow in from the pasture, and now he took time to relax.

His color-loving heart was filled with joy at the sight of the sky turning from azure blue to multiple shades of rose. Jack and Dutch strolled near the garden and looked carefully at the lettuce and carrot tops. As he surveyed the vegetables, his eye caught some greener plants' frazzled, nibbled edges. "Rabbits," Jackson hissed through gritted teeth. "They've come looking for food."

The grasslands were vast and open, as shadows cast various shapes on the ground, like cloud formations in the sky. The forest started showing its low bushes and tree sprouts on the far edge of the upland, where the heather grew more sparsely. Fully grown trees that stood there since Jackson's grandfather walked into the woods waved in the wind. A clearing emerged a few yards into the forest, where the canopy of the trees knitted together to form a vast umbrella of green. There was a knoll, or small hill, in the center.

Suddenly, Jackson was aware that someone or something was watching him. Dutch, calm and unruffled, didn't make a sound but raised his head and watched a movement with his deep brown eyes.

"Good evening, Jackson," a large red male deer nodded, speaking in the tones of an orator of great renowned.

Dutch was unimpressed, but Jackson was thunder-struck. The collie stayed in place but remained alert to his master's needs, ready to spring into action if necessary.

Jackson watched the deer but couldn't move. How could it happen? How could a deer speak? It was impossible. Jackson shook his head. "You did not speak to me," he finally insisted in disbelief.

"I imagined you would say that," the deer responded with a booming, rich accent. As the night breeze began to blow, the deer added, "Anyone can talk to an animal, but only Jackson Jones can hear the animal talk to him. For that ability alone, you are unique." The deer threw back his head and arched his massive neck. "You know the meaning of each bark Dutch makes. You laugh together, play together, and soothe his pain when he's bitten by a polecat. You understand each other well."

"Why are you speaking to me?" Jackson asked, attempting to understand. "Why are you speaking at all?"

The stately deer stretched his muscles. "I have heard you play your horn. As I stand in the hills above the village after the sun has set and the shadows have concealed your identity, I can hear every note. You are the one," he announced with confidence.

"The one what?" Jackson asked, confused.

"I heard the villagers talking," the deer confessed. "Your neighbors said the boy with the horn plays music that calms their souls. They fear the increasing strength of the Shaman's icy breath. The music of your horn soothes their fears. They said you can do anything."

"Anything?" Jackson asked, his eyes wide with surprise.

The mighty deer pawed at the ground with his front hoof. "You and your horn are heard. Certainly, you knew that."

"Yes, but no one in the village knows who is playing the music. Mr. No-name…only… *the boy with the horn.*"

Dutch observed the deer carefully. His eyes moved from the deer back to Jackson, following the conversation – always loyal, always ready.

The Monarch red deer stretched his sixteen antler tine points to the sky, displaying his mighty power. "Jackson, Dutch knows your name. It is…*Friend.*"

Jackson looked lovingly at his collie. "Yes, Dutch calls me *friend* each time he nuzzles my leg and follows my steps." He reached down and scratched behind the dog's ears. Then he asked the deer, "What is your name?"

"Some call me Mighty Red," the big one said modestly. "I'm just the "me" God intended me to be," he said as a soft expression filled his eyes. "I don't need to be more."

"But you have a name, and others use it," Jackson insisted. "When you're needed, they call you by your name, right?"

The mighty one's eyes softened. "Your friends in Waddyshire need you too, Jackson. They need the sweet sounds of your horn to calm their fears. In the mountains, the Shaman is restless. He roars into the night wind to frighten the villagers." The large deer's muscles trembled at the thought. "The Shaman-fey has more supernatural powers than any simple shaman. The eagle told me the Shaman-fey intends to blow until the village collapses. He is determined to avenge the death of his daughter."

"But the villagers had nothing to do with Fiona's death. The Shaman's daughter just got sick and died," Jackson insisted.

The deer drew closer as if to share a secret. "Since the Shaman-fey is a clairvoyant, it is said he heard some say, "Fiona died a deserved death.""

Jackson's face scowled. "But they didn't mean she deserved to die. They meant her death relieved her of her suffering since she was so sick."

Mighty Red shook his head. "The Shaman-fey doesn't see it that way." As Red warned, the wind began to pick up speed, bending the trees and whistling down the hills.

"He *chose* to see it differently," Jackson said bitterly. "He could have chosen to honor the caring attitude of his neighbors. But because his own heart was black with resentment and grief, he rejected the sympathetic attitude the villagers gave him.

"Some of us do that," Red agreed. "Regardless of the truth before us, we make all of life about ourselves and respond negatively to positive, simple life events."

Jackson squared his shoulders and set his jaw. "The Shaman's threats are not simple life events."

"No, they aren't," Red agreed. "What makes them complicated is our reaction to them."

Jackson patted his hand on his thigh, his signal for Dutch to follow him as he started back to his family's cottage. Dutch trotted along without a sound, never questioning, never doubting his master's commands.

"Your village friends need you, Jackson," Might Red called after him. "Their homes are being threatened by the fierce wind of the Shaman. They need to be at peace." Red's strong legs thumped on the forest floor. "You don't appreciate yourself, Jackson. You don't even accept that you are the one the villagers call for. You are the one, Jackson."

The sound of Mighty Red's words followed Jackson down the cobblestone road and back to town. Trees that grew beside the paving-stones, worn smooth by wagon wheels and horses' hoofs, swayed in the evening light.

Jackson remembered it all, what Red said, and his own doubt about the deer's words. Mighty Red was huge and majestic. The deer held his head high. Red's understanding voice was both commanding and filled with truth. Red told Jackson that he was "the one." Jack had no idea what he meant, but the big deer nearly convinced him that evening. He just had to figure out the one what.

Jackson felt the wind blow away the warmth of the day. High up the mountainside, where darkness hid the peak, a small glimmer of light and a delicate shimmer of smoke escaped from the Shaman's campfire. Jackson thought the evil one must be pacing back and forth as anger mounted inside him. Jack pulled his collar up around his neck.

When will your rage reach its peak? Jackson wondered if the Shaman-fey could hear his thoughts from so far up the slope. "The increasing strength of the wind tells me it won't be long until the speed of your squalls matches the evil in your heart."

Chapter Eight
At Home

Inside their thatched-roof cottage, the Jones family spent that summer evening at the heavy round table Pa made from logs he harvested from the forest. Mum placed the table near the open-hearth fireplace. Because of Pa's blacksmithing skills, the oven built in the brick wall to the side of the fire boasted a cast-iron oven door. During the summer, Jackson's mum used the cookstove to bake biscuits and cookies in the hours before the sun came up and heated the entire cottage.

That evening, after Jackson got home, the multi-pane windows and thick wooden doors of the cottage stood open to the fresh air. Jack, however, was beginning to feel a chill, even though his many activities usually kept him quite warm. Pa had laid some logs in the firebox and started a blaze to warm the room.

As the Shaman-fey continued to blow his angry, raw breath, Jackson's sister, Jemima, jumped up from her three-legged chair to close the door. Sitting beside the oil lamp, she strained to read her book. Jemima pulled her sweater more closely around her. "The wind might blow out the flame," she said. "Maybe I should dim the lamp. A little shorter flame may be safer. I think I can still read my book in the lower light. Can you see your handwork, Mummy?"

"I am most fine, Jemima, dear," Mum said as she threaded a different color of floss through the eye of her needle. "But, Jemima, it is already hard for you to see the words."

"I thought you wanted me to help you wind hanks of yarn into balls this evening," Jemima mused, bringing her small stool nearer to the light.

"Well, you're right, me-lassie," her mum said with a smile as she placed her embroidery in her lap. "We were going to wind some thick spun wool onto the skein counter and wrap them into balls. I like to have many lengths of yarn ready in the cupboard for kitting fine sweaters in the fall and winter. The weather is too warm to drape my knitting projects across my lap in the summer heat. But the embroidery and fancy needlework take my mind off the howling wind outside."

"Did we have supper, Mum?" Jackson asked as he scooted nearer the light coming from the fireplace. He was creatively whittling a deer that looked exactly like Mighty Red. Jackson flicked the chips from the carving into the fire. He was still wrestling with the truth of the day deep in his mind. Had he really held a conversation with a huge deer? Somehow, releasing the beautiful carving from the limewood made the encounter seem almost possible.

"Yes, Jack." His father took off his spectacles and studied the boy. "We had vegetable stew," he laughed. Folding his ledger book and placing it with his pencil in the secretary desk, Pa finished his work that began at five AM. Carefully maintaining the accounts of his blacksmithing and the items his wife used was his way of acknowledging that he had accomplished his goals for the day. He then felt a full measure of pride.

"Oh…right," Jackson paused and reflected on the evening. As the coldness of the Shaman's revenge cooled the house, the fire in the hearth warmed the floor's wide pine planks and made Jackson feel cozy and safe.

"Now, if you were to put some corn in the kettle," Pa suggested with his hand to his chin whiskers, "I would be happy to help you eat it. Bridget, I'll bet you would eat some, too."

"You'd win the Irish sweepstakes, Oliver," his wife answered with a laugh.

Soon the gathering room smelled like popped corn with the sweet addition of caramelized sugar and melted butter. Bridget folded her needle art and stored it in the cupboard where the salty corn couldn't touch it. Pa pulled pewter bowls from the shelves built into the bricks on the other side of the fireplace from the oven. He had turned the bowls on the lathe himself just the year before, using a flat disc of pewter. He shaped the discs into bowls with wide lips all the way out to the rolled brim.

While more corn popped, Jack shook the kettle to keep the kernels moving. His mind was still on Mighty Red.

"What have you been whittling this evening, son?" His pa asked as he looked again at the piece of wood with shaped corners and an emerging head.

"A deer," Jackson answered honestly. Still, Jack was not ready to tell why the deer was so important to him. "I saw a big one in the forest today. He had sixteen points."

"Very big, indeed," Pa agreed. Then he reached out and helped Jackson fill four bowls full of popcorn.

When they had eaten their fill of popcorn and emptied the kettle, Jackson took the heavy brass pot outside to the chickens and tossed the kernels. He squinted as salt from the hulls blew back in his face. As the wind continued to blow, Jackson darted quickly into the cottage. He finished cleaning the large kettle by wiping it out with hot water from the teakettle and a clean cloth. After drying the copper kitchen pot, it was placed on the fireplace burner to the right of the firebox to make sure it was stone-dry. Later, he would rehang it on the iron crane above the fireplace.

Jemima helped her mother wash and dry the bowls. Once they finished the evening activities, the family turned in, or that was the plan.

After his parents went to bed and his sister had settled for the night, Jackson pulled his golden horn from its leather bag and sat on the window seat facing the mountains. Dutch curled up silently beside him and placed his front paws on the boy's knee. Jackson spaced his teeth apart slightly, buzzed his lips, and put the horn to his mouth. Choosing only the sweetest note progressions, he blew love notes into the golden horn until his spirit lifted and floated on the melody of the songs. Who will hear his sweet lullabies? Who will know whose music rides on the wind? Will they say, "Yes, I hear the boy with the golden horn?" Or will they admit, "That is Jackson Jones, I hear?"

As he played his melody, Mighty Red's words hung on the notes and wedged their way into his mind. "You are the one," he heard the big deer repeat.

The boy paused in his music and searched the cloudy sky for any clue that would inform him about what the stag was saying. Clouds passed in front of the full moon and darkened the night around him. "Am I really the one?" he whispered as he strained to make sense of the pronouncement. "Who is trying to claim me? What is their purpose? What is mine?"

Tears gathered in the corners of his eyes and began to roll down his cheeks. Fear gripped his heart and caught in his throat. Another thought dared to fill him with dread.

"What did Mighty Red mean?" Jackson struggled to understand. "I may be *the one*. But, am I the *good* one or the *bad* one?"

Chapter Nine

Other Talents

For months, the nighttime hills echoed the magical melodies of Jackson Jones' horn. Since no one knew who played the graceful music in the gloaming, Jack didn't see it as any great accomplishment. He believed one had to impress others with their abilities to feel important. He received no recognition, no, "Thank you."

Mighty Red's pronouncement continued to amaze and confound Jackson. "You're the one, Jackson," echoed in his ears. Most days, villagers barely talked to him. Jackson walked around with his head down and didn't look anyone in the eye. Maybe that was the reason no one spoke. Jack appeared to be in another world. Admiration of the twilight musician was another thing. Everyone recognized the music as the mysterious horn player and admired his talent. They didn't seem to care what his name was. Jackson cared.

In the village square of Waddyshire sat a cluster of wooden tables and benches the people in the area had made.

It was a gathering place for friends and neighbors and a spot to sit and work in the shade of the trees. One evening Jackson sat at one of the painted tables in the shadow cast by a large oak tree, with his golden horn securely hidden in its pouch. The bag had a drawstring closure at one end, connected by another rope. It allowed him to carry the musical instrument over his shoulder. He always kept the sack with him when he was out and about. The horn was too valuable to leave at home. A thief might hear of the golden horn and break into the cottage to steal it. If someone asked about the ever-present sack, he would claim it was his paintbrushes. Cats and kittens that belonged to no one, but everyone claimed, scampered at his feet. That late day he sat painting a keepsake box his father helped him create.

Jackson had finished the foot-long box several days before. It was eight inches wide and eight deep, connected at the corners with perfect miters. He sanded it silky smooth, then painted it with black lacquer. The shiny black surface cured overnight. At his forge, his father created two decorative straps made of iron and a brass latch with a lock.

That evening Jackson began applying hand-painted flowers with red and yellow blossoms, using the horse-hair paintbrushes he made from a few strands of Champion's tail. He added a honey bee to one of the petals. The slim, sandy center of the bee, and black abdomen with its golden amber bands, looked realistic enough that honey might drip down the side. The box was indeed a thing of beauty. Jackson would take it and several other boxes he made into Lochlan to sell at the fair as soon as his father could get away from the forge.

Oliver would take an assortment of scythes, sickles, and sharp knives to sell at the bazaar-like fair. Bridget was particularly proud of her husband's tableware. The place settings, butterknives, forks, and spoons, were of the finest quality. Oliver also made buttons of brass in three sizes. The skilled blacksmith had created button molds with fine engravings on the top. Oliver would place a thin sheet of brass over the mold, press it down on the self-created reverse mold, and pop out the button caps onto the work table. Another mold created the bottom of the button. Then, Pa snapped the two pieces together. The small buttons went on fancy shoes and shirtwaists. A seamstress sewed medium buttons to children's coats. She affixed the large ones, with raised anchors, to military jackets and men's sweaters. Jemima's responsibility was to polish the buttons until they shone. For her work, she could buy a peppermint stick at the fair.

Jackson's mum loved the fair too and looked forward to it. They went into Lochlan at least once per year to sell their wares. Bridget would sell her artfully embroidered linens, pillowcases, and tea towels. Jackson's sister, Jemima, was young, but she also enjoyed participating in the outing regardless of the peppermint.

Several village neighborhood boys came around as Jack continued painting the box. In addition to the boys, Becky watched Jack paint. She had been Jackson's best friend since both began primary school. That evening, all those watching Jackson didn't talk. They watched in silence as the painted flowers seemed to grow and bloom. Jack believed the blossoms' aroma hung in the air.

Jackson noticed Becky's presence on the edge of the group. Even after a full day of helping her mother, Becky's white apron was still clean. Her bonnet hung down over her shoulders in a most becoming fashion. The hem of her full skirt was about eight inches off the floor, revealing her ankles wrapped in white cotton stockings.

The village friends stood breathlessly watching, mesmerized by the flowers' beauty with their opening petals. When Davy Hillagard opened his mouth to speak, he said nothing about the keepsake box or Jackson's skill in creating it.

"Me mum had a terrible headache last night." Davy put his hand to his forehead, rubbing it in sympathy. "Then she heard the night music."

"I heard the horn last night, too," Jackson admitted. Well, it was true. He couldn't help but hear the horn in his own hands.

The Vicar of Waddyshire stood a few yards back and smiled. "I heard the blessed music of the spheres too."

"Music of the spheres? What's that?" Davy's wrinkled face turned up with a generous amount of sauciness.

"Can you tell him, Jackson?" the Vicar asked.

"Well," Jack looked from one of his friends to another. Would they think he was bragging if he revealed his knowledge?

"Jackson?" Vicar Turner prompted.

Jack's eyes remained on his art. "A mathematician once said that God created the first music. He said, 'When the Lord God moved the planets and stars around in the heavens, the vibrations made as the heavenly bodies passed, created music.'" Jack's gaze was low, where emotions live. Then he looked up and caught Becky's smile.

Davy's eyes squinted as he smirked. "Did the horn sound like heavenly music to you, Jackson?"

"Yes…I guess."

Davy snickered. "Who was the angel that played it?"

"I…I…" Jackson stammered. He almost denied his own identity. He closed his mouth and gritted his teeth. "I guess it was a toothless recluse from the forest."

Becky choked on the description. "Sorry," she apologized as she looked to her right and left. "You mean someone like Digger Jinx?"

"Maybe," Jackson agreed until the image of the cemetery worker and the man from the top of his roof jarred his senses. Digger had one missing, yellow front tooth, just as described. Most of the village folk crossed to the other side of the road when Digger went by.

"Are ya saying you believe in angels, Jackie Boy?" Davy asked with a sneer on his face.

"Are you saying you don't?" The Vicar blurted out.

Jackson squirmed in his seat. "I haven't seen one," Jackson admitted. "But, sure as Bob's-your-uncle, I believe angels exist."

Chapter Ten

All are Needed

"Jackson Jones, the school had many lectures on the primitive belief in spiritual beings." Headmaster Billett had paused to listen to the discussion of angels and watch Jackson apply paint to the keepsake box. Billett heard it all.

Vicar Turner nearly fell over when he pulled himself up straight from the tree he leaned on. "Headmaster," he snapped. "No more blasphemous talk against the teachings of the church. Be in my office tomorrow." He started to turn but paused and asked, "What have I taught about fearing the Shaman, David Hillagard?"

"Uh…" Davy was lock-jawed.

"Mr. Hillagard? What have I said?"

"Uh…pray?" he stammered.

"I should think you could remember that part," the Vicar spit out. "Mr. Jones, what have I said about fear?"

"The three Ps: pray…palaver…perform," Jack blushed.

"Yes, me laddie," the Vicar said with an encouraging smile. "*Pray* to the good Lord; *palaver,* talk to others about it; and *perform,* put a plan into action. Now, the night musician has put a plan of soothing music into action. Mr. Billett, what have you done?" The Vicar didn't even wait for an answer. He turned on his heels and stormed away.

Everyone in the group gasped. Vicar Turner verbally whipped their teacher. The headmaster blushed and cleared his throat.

At that moment, Oliver Jones locked up his forge for the evening. Seeing Oliver walk over, Billett used him to draw attention from himself. He nodded at Oliver and smiled sheepishly. "Jackson always did a masterful job in school, Oliver."

"Did you tell him how much you liked his work, Headmaster?" Oliver asked. He knew Jack's teacher never recognized him for his perfectly drawn pictures or correct Mathematics. Jack's beautiful paragraphs of flawless prose never hung with pride on the Excellence-in-Pedagogy board at the back of the classroom.

"Well, of course, we expected more from Jackson," the headmaster defended his position. "His work was always perfect, and he came from such a creative family. The other students were the ones who needed encouragement."

"His work was perfect indeed," Oliver spoke crisply. "But Jack didn't know it inside, where confidence begins. He never heard it from you, or anyone for that matter, except his mum and me."

"You wouldn't want him to boast," the instructor corrected quickly.

"Self-esteem is not a flaw, Headmaster," Oliver spoke in clear tones the teacher could not misunderstand. "Those who feel good about themself and their work can see the beauty God gave them. They do not esteem themselves to be better than others. They begin to see their gifts as avenues that make them *equal* to others and their talents. God gives everyone gifts, Headmaster. Some are more visible than others. Little Jemima has a talent for making others feel comfortable. That is a special ability."

Headmaster Billett nodded slowly. "I will consider that," which was an unusual statement for the headmaster. He seemed to have a talent for knowing everything, or at least he seemed to think he did. Rarely did he value others' ideas. Billett turned toward his cottage beside the schoolhouse, then paused and put his hand on Jackson's shoulder. "Your keepsake box is exquisite, Jackson." He patted the boy on the back and moved on down the road.

"I never heard him say anything like that before, Pa," Jackson blushed.

"Perhaps the teacher still has things to learn," Oliver said with a smile.

The village boys who gathered around said nothing. They never did. Perhaps they didn't know how to recognize another person's good work. Still, to their credit, they didn't put Jackson down or belittle his work either.

Becky bent low and whispered in Jack's ear, not wanting the others to hear her words. "Your box is magnificent, Jackie."

"Thank you, Becky," he whispered. As fireflies began to dart around the yard, waiting for darkness to reveal their light, Jackson started to gather his brushes and paints.

"Mum will ring the dinner bell soon," Davy sighed as he watched Jackson fold up for the evening. "I'm hungry."

"Me too," Jackson admitted. "I'll bet your family will be eating that large rabbit you trapped this morning, Davy. You are an excellent hunter/trapper."

"Thank you, Jackson. Do you hunt?"

"No," Jackson mumbled with his head hung low. To his mind, it was just another thing he couldn't do. "You have all the talent for putting food in the pot. My family would starve if they had to depend on arrows from my quiver or meat from my traps."

"I guess your pops was right, Jackson." Davy's eyes brightened as if he had learned a secret. "We all have talents, and all our talents are needed."

Jackson placed the keepsake box in the wooden wagon he had owned since he was a small child. Pa had made the wagon with wood he had harvested when the wind blew down the pine tree near the barn door. The wagon had a suspension capable of carrying precious cargo around town without fear that bumps and ruts would damage the merchandise. Jackson wondered if the deer had mistaken him for his father. His pa was more than a blacksmith. The talents of Jack's father were unique and many. At the bellows and forge, he was the one who created objects beyond usual patterns and shapes. Oliver was a craftsman in his trade. Jack knew his father could do anything.

Chapter Eleven

And the Wind Blew

That night the wind blew across the heath and rustled through the tall trees. It sounded like the Shaman had nearly reached top velocity. His blowing would finally do terrible damage to the village. Jackson could feel the frosty breeze grow colder despite the late summer date. Jack sat in the moonlight of his bedroom window and blew his horn. He knew the music brought healing joy to those close enough to hear. However, the more he blew out songs of praise, the colder it got. What was happening?

Everyone in Jackson's house was asleep. Even Dutch lay motionless on the blue braided, rag floor mat beside Jack's bed. Jemima had ripped some old fabric into strips and helped her mother braid the long pieces into a rug. Jackson looked out the window as the wind blew the trees, bending them low. Winter would be coming in a matter of months. Jackson had grown during the summer and knew his winter boots and coat would be tight. The Shaman's icy breath had changed the weather in the shire. It was a strange mix of summer and winter on the same day. But Jackson believed he had to go out into the night, find the Shaman, and stop him.

"Dutch." Jackson quietly nudged the dog on the top of his head. "Come on," he commanded as he slipped out of bed.

Dutch watched as the boy yanked his long breeches off a wall peg and pulled them on. The two wool sweaters his mum had made were on a shelf beside the hooks. First, he put on the gray one with the thick cable needlework and then the black sweater, hoping the layers would keep him warm. When he grabbed his boots off the floor, there was still a pair of wool socks tucked inside. He wondered if his feet would fit if he put on a second pair of stockings. He had to try. The temperature outside dropped by multiple degrees in the early nighttime hours. If Jackson did nothing, neighbors who were already asleep could awaken to a freezing house.

His mum had knitted a stocking cap during the previous winter. Jackson had to stop and remember where he had put it. Snapping his fingers when the location came to mind, he hurried to the cabinet in the gathering room, pulled out the middle drawer, and removed the cap and matching gloves. With his golden horn secured in its pouch, Jack reached for the shepherd's staff that leaned against the wall in the corner. Then, he slipped out the door into the frigid night with Dutch at his heels.

Jackson had heard recent reports of wolf packs roaming the hills. Usually, he might not be afraid of wolves, but with the flash freezing from the icy breath of the Shaman, wolves in need of food might not keep their distance. Family milk cows and pets could be in danger. Also, Mighty Red may not be safe. Deer meat is a wolf's favorite celebration meal. If deer or moose isn't around, another meat will have to do. Some hunters said ten or twelve wolves surrounded them when hunting in the woods. Jackson was sure Dutch would be his protection from the night prowlers. But Jack also knew, Dutch was large enough to be a meal for several wolves to share.

Moonlight on the road lit the path as if by many lanterns. Jackson thought about the advantage of the light, then remembered the opposite side of seeing his surroundings, being visible to other hungry eyes. Trudging through the cold, the pebbles beneath his feet popped and crunched like on a winter night. A few cottages still had lit lamps in the window. He wondered if some villagers were up trying to warm their homes by laying a fire in the fireplace.

A pebble-covered forest path entered the woods from the village's main cobbled road. The earthy, musky smell of heather was subtle and pleasant. Jackson turned there and slowly took steps past the low plants and bushes before entering the area with the tall trees. The farther he ventured into the forest, the darker his surroundings. The light could not filter through the denser stand of trees. Dutch stayed beside Jackson with every step, growling softly, shifting his gaze from side to side.

Both Jackson and the dog knew someone or something was stalking them. The boy could feel it. He assumed wolves tracked their path. With Dutch's nose in the air, sniffing every scent, the dog seemed to smell danger— wolf, fox, or man, it mattered not. Small twigs snapped too near to be comfortable. Whatever was there in the rapidly growing darkness, it was close by.

Jackson turned around quickly and jumped. Another lantern swung along the path behind him. "Who is there?" Jack's voice was firm.

"Jackie, it's me."

"Becky? What are you doing? It's dangerous out here." Jackson walked back, holding his lantern high.

"I saw you pass the house and got worried." She placed her free hand under her armpit to keep it warm.

"Worried?" Jackson shook his head in disbelief. "Now, I will worry about your being out in the cold where wolves may be roaming."

"Jackson Jones, if you can worry about me, I can worry about you. I am going with you tonight unless you want me to walk back home by myself."

"That's not fair, Becky." He thought about the horn that hung over his shoulder. No one knew who played the music of the night. How would he confront the Shaman with his magical melodies if no one was supposed to know who played them? If Becky were there, she would find out.

"Not fair?" Becky stomped her foot. "Jackson, what is going on?"

"I cannot tell you," he insisted.

"Why? You tell me everything, and I tell you the same."

"It's not fair because you're putting me in an uncomfortable spot." Jack thumped the shepherd's staff into the ground beside him.

"How?" Becky demanded as she pulled on Jackson's coat sleeve. "I don't even know what you're saying. How can I put you in a bad position? That would mean I know your secret, and I'm using it to manipulate you." She stuffed her hand in her pocket and scowled. The lamplight revealed her confusion.

"Becky," Jackson began, "if I tell you, it could put you and your family in danger, too."

"Why?" She lowered her lantern and walked closer. "What are you not telling me?" Becky turned the palm of her hand up in surrender. "Jackie…talk to me."

Jackson's shoulders slumped as he struggled to know what to say. "Pa said not to tell anyone." He moaned, torn between telling and keeping his secret. He and Becky shared everything they had ever thought about since they were six years old. He looked away for a moment. "I was in the forest about four months ago." He pulled the pouch from his shoulder and balanced the staff against a nearby tree. Reaching inside the leather bag, he carefully removed the horn. A fine stream of moonlight filtered down through a few trees, setting the instrument aglow.

"That is beautiful, Jackie," Becky choked as she spoke. "Are you telling me that thing was in the forest?"

"I am," Jackson whispered. "I found it there."

Becky just stared at him. "I don't know what to say. I would never have dreamed that you found that in the woods."

"I did," he admitted.

Becky's mouth dropped open. "No one in the village band has a horn that shines like that one. It doesn't even look like brass," she said as she started to reach for it.

"Sorry, you can't hold it," Jackson pulled the horn back and apologized again. "Really, I am sorry, Becky."

"Is it spirit-smacked, Jackie?" Becky laughed as she put her hand on her hip. Suddenly, her smile faded when Jackson's expression didn't change. She rubbed her arms. "Jackie, this all sounds serious."

"Something like that," he said with a smile, trying to convince Becky that the horn's enchantment was a trivial thing. "Pa said the horn belonged to his grandpa. He said, 'you don't learn to play this horn. The horn chooses the player.'" Jackson turned and started to walk again. "Now, you'd better go home. I'll find the Shaman and make him stop freezing our people in Waddyshire."

"How are you going to make him stop, Jackie?" Becky's tone was playfully sassy. "Throw your horn at him?"

"Not the horn. Just the music." He answered and then eyed her carefully.

"Oh, sure, and it's the music that will bring him to his knees," she mocked with a grin.

Jackson shook his head slowly. "Right. But it won't be safe for you." He stole another glance at Becky, hoping to see a clue if she believed him.

"What do you mean, Jackie?" She demanded with a stomp of her foot. "You're not making any sense."

"Becky…I," he stuttered and stammered, "I have been playing the most beautiful music I can. But," he stopped and tried to gather the right words. It was hard to explain the strange circumstances and the monster's reaction to the music. "The Shaman wants Waddyshire to freeze until the solid ice crumbles under his hate. So, playing sweet melodies reinforces his evil desires and brings more destruction to the shire. I'll have to find the saddest, most painful note progressions. Since the most heartfelt sounds brought out his evil nature, hopefully, music of pain and suffering will slow his carnage and calm his heart."

Becky's mouth opened in stunned amazement. "You have been playing? You? On that horn at night?"

"You cannot tell a living soul," he insisted with his hand on Becky's arm. "It's not me. It's the horn, a golden horn."

"Gold?" Becky gasped.

"Hush. It is very valuable. If the word gets around that we have a large piece of gold at our cottage, someone might try to break in and steal it." He waved the horn around quickly. "I must find the Shaman. Becky, please, go home." He started into the forest again and then stopped.

In a small clearing further into the woods, where the moonlight lit the space again, the boy saw multiple pairs of eyes beginning to encircle them. A pack of wolves surrounded them, blocking their escape if they had wanted to flee. Snarling wolves with gnashing teeth, their heads down, hunched in an attack stance, glared out of the darkness. Jack turned around and checked. Becky had not turned back. A few paces behind him, Becky froze in fear at the terrifying sight in front of her.

Dutch barked ferociously and quickly jumped around the clearing, aggressively staring down each of the wolves. Jackson thrust the shepherd's staff out in front of them while Dutch crouched like a tiger.

"Oh, Jackie." Becky's voice cracked in fear as she whispered his name. "What will we do?"

"Don't move," Jackson said firmly through his teeth. "If we run, we'll look like prey. Wolves love to hunt."

Chapter Twelve

Eyes that Stare

Becky couldn't take her eyes off the wolf pack. Her silence concealed a scream. The snarling animals were ferocious, their bared teeth ready to attack. Becky whispered, "Blimey!"

"Look away from them, Becky. Your eye contact is challenging to them." Jackson spoke softly. He slowly turned away and looked at the trees.

Along with Dutch, the three of them became a defense team. It didn't matter that there were no sheep to protect. The wolves were hungry enough to attack anything. What mattered was the superior strength of the boy, his dog, and Jackson's belief that they were in control of the night.

Slowly, Jackson brought the horn to his lips. He thought for a moment about what to play. Then, it came to him. All he had to offer was his breath through the horn and the thoughts in his head. He had to make Becky, him, and

Dutch look scary. Like they were the ones to fear. He knew the somber tones would hurt Becky and Dutch's ears. They would have to withstand that threat. Still, the aggressive sound of the mournful music was better than the wolves tearing them apart. Jack took a deep breath. He might have only one chance to frighten the wolves. They may quickly see that he was only a boy with a horn.

He pursed his lips tightly and blew as hard as he could. A piercing melody burst forth from the horn's bell and split the silence of the night. Calming, soothing tones relaxed the wolves.

Whimpering like an injured pup, each wolf peeled off from the pack and slumped into the night. Jackson finally relaxed his hold on the horn and stood up straight. Reaching out for Becky, he threw his arm around her.

Just as the danger from the wolf pack passed, Jackson spotted two more eyes glaring at them from the darkness. Fixed from a point above his gaze, a fiery evil bloke loomed over them like a menacing giant. It had to be the Shaman-fey.

Becky followed Jack's gaze until she was staring into the eyes of evil. In the blackness of the night, all they could see was the glint and clash of hate.

Jackson blinked, trying to focus better, but he couldn't make out any more of the figure. *Who was he?* Jack reached out, took Becky by her hand, and tugged, pulling her closer. He whispered, "Tear off a piece from the bottom of your petticoat and quickly stuff the cloth in your ears."

With her eyes fixed on the glowing black holes in what should be the Shaman's face, Becky reached up and tore a little piece of the ruffle from the top of her white pinafore. Just as she ripped it into two smaller pieces and put a wad in each ear, Jack put the horn to his lips.

If the notes that mellowed the villagers in Waddyshire, filling them with joy, gave the Shaman the strength to blow a frosty wind for weeks, Jackson would have to try the reverse effect. Or, the ice would overtake the village and drop the summer temperatures into frigid numbers.

Jackson forced his brain to think again about things that made him sad and doubt himself. He began to play the most sorrow-filled tunes he had ever played to get the Shaman to surrender his evil hold on the shire.

The evil one had never come into the village. No one had seen the beast, yet here he stood, challenging Jackson, masked by the darkness of the night.

As the sliver of a moon appeared through a small break in the clouds, Jack could see grey, shabby strips of rags hanging from the stooped figure's shoulders. Jackson wondered if once the evil one wore an elegant dress coat. His hair looked long, matted, and dirty in the dim light. At one time, it was probably wavy. Filth covered his face and hands, crusting over him like a full-body camouflage suit. The sulfuric stench of evil filled the forest glade causing Jackson and Becky to gag.

Icicles hung from the creature and glistened like ghastly jewels, the remanence of weeks of breathing the frigid air. The Shaman's stiffly frozen arms could not strike out against Jack and Becky. He gasped, desperately trying to conjure up his only weapon, the icy wind. Gagging and choking, not even a tiny spritz of sleet spewed from his mouth.

Dutch stood at the ready. The size of the great brick of ice did not deter him. He growled and crouched low.

Jackson had just minutes to act. If the Shaman had time to start thawing, he might be warm enough to attack again. Jack had played calming, uplifting music for weeks to soothe the monster. But it didn't work as the icy wind continued to blow.

Hopefully, Jack's reverse approach would work. Jackson saw how the sad tune affected his father when he first brought the horn home. He was afraid the mournful music would make the whole village sick. But Jack had no choice. He had to weaken the Shaman's power. Jackson stared into his eyes while the beast-of-a-man stood like a grotesque ice sculpture. He would not be the first to blink.

With white wads of cloth sticking out of her ears, Becky was as ready as she could be. Jackson hoped she would cup her hands over her ears once he started playing.

He thought of all the sad images he could remember with his horn to his lips. Visions of Headmaster Billett's feeble excuse to his father about why he never told Jackson he was a good worker drooped before his eyes. The blank faces of village boys, gathered around his construction of keepsake boxes in silence, hurt his heart. Last spring, Jack won first place in the spelling bee just weeks before his eighth-year graduation. His medal lay buried at the back of the school's trophy case. The neglected award brought up aches so deep they turned his stomach. All those sad thoughts were stuffed into Jackson's soul and lay there at the base of his own resentment. Then, like a lightning bolt, he added the evil one's grief.

The Jones family had lost a boy, too, Jack's younger brother, Henry. When Henry died last year of influenza, he was only ten years old. Jackson saw how it affected his whole family. He put the horn to his lips and thought of the grief that filled their house, making the air so heavy it seemed to smother everyone inside. Jack could see his mother's face and salty tears that would not stop flowing in his memory. He felt her pain, like a knife that pierced his heart and would not let him breathe. His father pounded on iron all night long in the forge, flattening it, folding it, and flattening it again until he was ready to quench the blade.

Plaintive moans came from the horn and filled the forest clearing with tears. Jackson's eyes held the demon's gaze, burning a hole inside him until Jack felt the Shaman's soul merge with his. On and on, Jack played his sad tale of anguish and suffering. Without his family and Becky, he would have been a phantom, the nobody-boy of Waddyshire. Without Fiona, the Shaman became utterly forsaken.

At the wail of the horn, the Shaman melted in front of them, doubled over, and stumbled at Jackson's feet. Puddles of ice and tears gathered around the Shaman. The notes Jackson chose were the sad ones, not the angry ones. Jackson's heart was breaking inside the melody that filled the woods.

Beside him on the ground, Becky was sobbing as softly as possible. Jackson felt bad about the sadness his notes sent down into the village. Everyone in Waddyshire had suffered enough already from the recent ice and the fear that came with it.

When the Shaman could no longer stay on his feet, Jackson crumpled at the same time. With his small snippet of remaining energy, Jackson shoved the horn into the pouch, drew the string closed, and struggled to get back up. Jack knew he'd have to get Becky away from the filthy wretch while the Shaman, weakened by his own misery, could not fight back. Jackson had not defeated him, but the Shaman's efforts slowed to a thaw.

"Jackson, it's as you said." Becky's eyes grew large with amazement. "If there is only hate, the person withers and dissolves away."

Quickly, Jackson snatched Becky off the ground, jerked up his staff, and raced out of the forest, back onto the path leading into the village. Once they were home, Becky gave Jack a little hug before running up to her front door. Jackson jumped onto his front porch, gently lifted the latch, then silently slipped back into the house. By morning, the temperature in the gathering room had warmed.

Chapter Thirteen

He Came with a Message

Jackson stood near the fire and worked the bellows in the brick fireplace of his father's forge. The bellows blew air into the fire to increase the heat in the flame. The temperature needed to rise to 2150-2375 degrees. Any blacksmith was careful not to get the fire so hot that the steel would melt or too low to prevent the steel from bending. The iron turned red when the steel was hot enough to shape. Pumping the bellows wasn't a hard job. But, so close to the fire, Jackson felt like a loaf of his mum's bread, baking a little more each day. Mostly, he enjoyed spending time with his father. And Dutch loved spending time with them both. The dog lay at the door on the cool earthen floor where he could catch any breeze that came his way.

"We're fixing the wheel on Archie Hampton's buggy," Oliver said. He wiped his hands on his long, leather apron, already soiled with a lifetime of work. The blacksmith apron had a split in the middle, allowing Oliver to cradle

Champion's leg when he fitted the horse's shoes. "Fetch me a cup of water, please, Son."

Jackson took the long-handled tin cup from where it hung on a wall peg. After dipping it in the wooden bucket that sat in the coolest corner of the forge, he handed it to his father. "Here, Pa," he offered.

Oliver gulped the water, handed Jack the cup, then put the curved iron back in the flame. He used long heavy tongs to hold Archie's new metal wheel rim in the fire. In a short time, Oliver pulled the red-hot metal from the flame and moved it quickly to the two-hundred-pound anvil that sat proudly in the middle of the room. After a few heavy whacks of the hammer, he studied the shape of the broken rim, then quenched it in the water to complete the creation.

From outside came a shrill shriek. It caused Dutch's ears to stand up straight.

"It's all right, Dutch," Jack assured him. "Let's go check."

"That's fine, Jack," his pa offered. "I shouldn't need the bellows anymore. I think I have the right curve to the wheel rim already."

"Thanks, Pa." Jackson held Dutch's collar, stepped outside, and peeked around the corner. Something had caused the fear-filled scream. Jack didn't know if someone was in danger or if the sound was that of children laughing and playing in the village square. He stepped a little farther out onto the cobblestones. The collie dog followed, step by step, then stopped and growled in the direction of the trees.

"Jackie!" Becky shrieked as she ran from the woods and into the open land on the edge of the village. Birds, pecking at the ground, jumped, and fluttered from their feist of low scattered seeds. "Jackson Jones!" she yelled again and bent low as if frozen in place, gasping.

Children in the square had built tents out of their mum's old coverlets by draping them over the tables under the trees. When they heard the yelling, they popped their heads out of the tent's opening to see what happened. Several family dogs, asleep on the front step of their homes, stood with hunched backs and bared teeth, growling at the sound of danger.

Jack ran from the side of his father's forge, scanned the horizon, and frantically dashed off toward the stand of trees near Geoffrey Kirby's granary business. Lifting Becky off the ground, Jackie threw his arms around her. "What's wrong?" he asked, choking on the fear that gripped him.

Becky's face, streaked with a strange mix of tears and fear, twitched with excitement. She grabbed Jackson's shirt and danced frantically in front of him. Several days had passed since Jackson blew the mournful dirge that softened the Shaman's heart and stopped the icy wind. Now, Becky was upset and fearful again. Hadn't fear passed?

Billy Busby threw his fists to his hips and stared off in Jack's direction. "Hey, let go of Rebecca," he demanded.

Becky stared back at Billy in surprise. She called out quickly. "I'm fine. I, I fell."

"Go home, Billy," Jackson ordered. "Your mum is looking for you." He stared at his neighbor, then stomped his foot in the boy's direction as if startling a stray cat.

"You sure you're all right, Becky?" Billy asked, hesitating before turning.

"Yes," she answered as she clung to Jackson's arm. "I am fine." She looked up at Jack and yelled at Billy. "I fell, but I'm okay. Nothing's broken. Nothing's even bruised. Go home, Billy. It's almost mealtime."

Billy pointed his finger at the two and snapped back, "I will. But you go home too, Rebecca Hampton, or I'm telling your mum."

"I'm going," she cracked. Becky whispered with a sass, "Billy Busby, you're not my pa."

Not hearing what Rebecca said, Billy turned and headed for home while Jack put his arm around Becky's shoulder as they walked to her cottage. When Billy got to his house, he went in, then peered out the window.

"He's still peeking out at us," Becky giggled.

"You make him no never-mind," Jackson reassured her with a sideways hug. He stopped, turned her around, and asked, "Becky, why were you screaming for me?"

"I was in the forest, gathering wildflowers," she gasped as a memory crossed her face. "I press them between the pages of a thick book until they dry. Then, I put them in an airtight crock with floral and citric scents for twenty-four hours. I make little potpourri bags from the fragrant leaves to put in clothing drawers or on the window sill at home. I plan to sell some of the bags at the fair."

Jackson looked at Becky as his face scrunched in confusion and curiosity. "That's why you yelled, Becky? Did you fall into a flower bed? Did you get scratched on rose thorns?"

"No," Becky stretched out the "nooo" to make a point. "There was a deer, a gigantic animal. He, he," she stammered for a second, then continued. "Jackie, you will downright think I'm daft."

"Why? You are the least daft person I know," Jackson laughed and hugged her again.

"Jackie…the big deer … talked to me." Becky dropped her head to her chest. "He did, Jackson. Indeed, he did."

Jack held his breath. "What did the deer look like?" He stopped, threw his head back, and whispered to himself. *Jackson Jones, how many deer do you know that talk to themself?*

Becky snapped her head back and pulled on his shirt. "What?" she asked him with narrowed eyes. "Just how many deer do *you* know that can talk?"

"A big red one," he admitted. "He's called Mighty Red."

"Well, he asked me to give you a message," she hissed as she turned her back on Jack and squared her shoulders.

"A message? He talked to you and wanted you to tell me something?" Jack grabbed her shoulders and spun her around. "Did he say anything about 'the one?'"

"The one what?" she asked skeptically.

"Never mind," Jack stuttered. "What did he want you to tell me?"

Becky shook her head in disbelief. She looked down at the bonnet she had taken off and carried upside down, using it as a cloth basket for her blossoms. "It will dizzy your mind, Jackie. It was from Mother Goose." Becky raised her hand in a pledge. "I am telling the truth. I hope it makes sense to you. The deer said, 'tell Jackson this rhyme.'

Ride a cock horse to Banbury Cross,
To see a fine lady upon a white horse;
Rings on her fingers and bells on her toes,
And she shall have music wherever she goes."

Jackson almost laughed. But then, he had to admit a fact. When Mighty Red first spoke to him, it all seemed unbelievable to him, too. Why not a talking deer that can also read? "I know you're not daft, and neither am I. So, the deer must be the one with a head full of feathers," Jackson held his ground firmly.

"Hey," Billy yelled from his door. "You two best be getting home."

Becky groaned, "I am home." She dismissed Billy with a wave of her hand as she stood near her front gate. "Mind your own self, Billy," she demanded.

"Mother Goose?" Jackson whispered hoarsely and nearly choked on a laugh. "Where would a wild animal get a book of nursery rhymes?"

Becky looked at him with a half-smile and shook her head. "It's fine if the deer talks? As long as he doesn't quote a nursery rhyme?" She shook her head again. "I don't believe it." She brushed off her skirt and straightened her pinafore. "I have no idea what to think. And I sure don't know what his rhyme means?" Then she wrinkled her nose. "Jackie, that is not the only issue. That deer talked, and that's the bigger miracle. Now, Jackson Jones, you talk to me."

"I know, Becky. I didn't tell you," Jackson admitted. "But I also know I have no idea what the deer was talking about." He patted Becky on the shoulder as she turned to go into her cottage. Jackson thought. *I have no idea what it means. We're going to the fair in Lochlan. We're not even going to Banbury. Banbury Cross is on the River Cherwell in Oxfordshire, That's more than fifty miles from Lochlan.*

Chapter Fourteen

Emma

Jackson slowly walked on toward his cottage, puzzling about the whole situation. He stepped up to the front door, then waved at Becky. She seemed to be looking at something near the woods. Jack watched as Becky didn't go inside but began to hurry across the village square.

"Becky?" he whispered in a husky call after her. He didn't want to get Billy Busby stirred up again.

She turned and waved in a great circle indicating Jack should follow her.

What is she doing? Jack wondered. "Rebecca Hampton…wait!" Then he saw what had captured Becky's attention. She was following Emma Walker, a four-year-old who shouldn't wander about alone.

Emma wasn't running. She ambled along in pursuit of her new puppy, Baby Dog. Jack was introduced to the pup when he neared her house that morning. Emma had only the

Lazy Lamb Lunchroom, then General Granger's General Store to pass before she disappeared into the open land of the heath.

"Emma," Becky called out. Her voice sounded full of fun. Then, Emma seemed to respond as she slowed a little. Becky turned when she heard Jack approach from behind. With Jackson darting up quickly, she threw her hand behind her and waved for him to move slowly.

Jackson stuffed his hands in his pockets and slowed his pace to a relaxing stroll. "Well, hi there, Emma," he said. "Where are you going?"

"Baby Dog got away," she whispered with her bottom lip sticking out.

Becky gently put her hand on Emma's shoulder. "You know a little swan may sit on your lip if it's sticking out, don't you? You know King Wilber is the Seigneur of the Swans."

Emma brushed an imaginary swan off her mouth. "The King is what?"

Rebecca motioned for Jack to get Baby Dog before the puppy escaped into the tree line farther up the hills. Becky continued to soothe the little one. "The King is in charge of all the swans in the country."

"I saw the little dog squirt past," Digger droned from the roof of General Granger's store. "Been watchin' Emma, too. She's a little cutie," he added with a smarmy tone. "I can see everyone from up here."

"I'd think you could," Becky agreed as she searched the village square for everyone Digger Jinx could stalk from his bird's eye view of the village. There were children everywhere on Waddyshire Square. Some laughed as they hung upside down from the best tree branches in the village. Several read books in the shade as they leaned against a gnarled tree trunk. The Orme twins were in a foot race, competing opposite each other as they always did. Becky nudged Jackson and nodded in the children's direction.

Suddenly, Jackson's stomach felt squeamish. What was it about Digger that made Jackson not trust him? Was it his dirty appearance? Jackson's father got hot and grimy from standing in front of the fire in the forge. But Oliver Jones washed and put on clean clothes for the evening.

Jinx had a reason for some of his dirt. Certainly, digging a six-foot hole in the soil would make anyone filthy. Climbing on a roof to stitch in new long strands of dusty, dried water reeds would also be a dirty job. The filth that covered Digger ground in so much, it buried itself in the skin of his arms and face. Jackson cringed and tried to distract Emma from the shabby, dirty gravedigger.

"Look what I have," Jack said as he held out the tiny golden pup.

"My Baby Dog!" Emma squealed as she reached for her puppy.

"Why don't you let Jackson carry her for you?" Becky soothed. "We'll want to get you home before wandering off again." She paused as Emma began to drag her feet.

"No…I want to carry Baby Dog." Emma demanded as she reached for the dog. "She's mine."

Baby Dog was a Yorkshire terrier, a feisty, brave, and often bossy tiny pup. Jackson saw the little bundle of fur making demands on everyone that morning. "Baby Dog," he laughed, "you think you're big and mighty."

The puppy pointed her little ears straight up and cocked her head. Staring at Jack, Baby Dog barked in a high-pitched, yappy sound.

"Well now," Rebecca stared back at the four-year-old girl, locking eyes with the little one. "Just what is this all about, Emma?" Baby Dog snapped her mouth closed and twisted her head from side to side. "Just what I thought," Becky cooed at the little dog with a silky coat of steel blue and rich golden tan. "All bark and no fight." She reached out with her palm turned up under the puppy's jaw. "You are a cutie."

"Play your horn, Jackie," Becky urged. "Now that the dog has settled down, Emma will calm down too if you play it."

"But everyone will hear me." Jack pulled the rope on the leather pouch even tighter, protecting the golden horn.

"Oh…" Becky paused, "right."

Jackson relaxed and smiled. "You can convince her, Becky. You have a real talent for talking with people, young or old."

"Jackie, don't be daft," Becky protested. "Talking isn't a talent."

"Of course, it is," Jackson laughed. "Do you think Billy Busby could convince anyone of anything?" Jack nearly choked on a muffled laugh. "Wait, he could convince people to hurry home to whitewash their cat, just to get away from him. Billy has no more personality than a handful of raw wool."

"What do you think, Emma?" Becky asked as she reached down to the child. Putting her hand under the child's chin, she tipped it up to bring Emma's eyes to meet hers. "You were such a brave girl to go after your Baby Dog. I'll bet you're tired. I would be happy to carry you," she offered.

"Well…" Emma began. "I'm not a baby. I am tired, though."

Becky started to laugh and pursed her lips. "Of course, you're not a baby." She offered Emma her hands. "Come on," she said as she took the child in her arms and carried Emma home.

At her cottage, Willodean Walker burst out the door. "Emma, where…?"

"Her dog ran off, Ma'am." Becky handed Emma over to her mother. "I saw her heading toward the woods and went after her."

"Becky has a way with people," Jackson added again.

"Oh my, yes. Becky, all of the children love you."

"They do?" Rebecca stammered.

"Even Mrs. Fussy said you were special. When her chest hurt terribly, and she couldn't stand up, she said you stayed by her side and calmed her until the practical nurse arrived." Mrs. Walker grabbed Becky in a big hug. "You may have saved Emma's life just like you did for Mrs. Fussy."

"Thank you, Mrs. Walker," Becky said as she started down the porch step.

"Bless you, child." Willodean raised her hand in the sign of a blessing, then closed the door.

Jackson walked Becky home again, this time much slower and closer. "See, Becky, talent isn't captured in a horn or at the end of a pen. Even though blessed with talent, people often let others decide the value of the gift. But God ranks all talents as equally good."

Becky shook her head in puzzlement. "How do you know that, Jackie?"

Jack thought for a moment and shrugged. "I don't know. Sometimes things just spill out of my mouth. Don't know where they come from."

Becky stepped up on the large entry stone at her house. "So…the deer said you are *the one,* but we don't know, 'the one what.' Maybe we are all *the one,* the right one needed for the job at hand."

Chapter Fifteen

Planning

A few weeks later, Jackson, his family, and Dutch started early in the morning for the fair in Lochlan. Champion trotted behind, tethered to the back. Becky, her family, several other neighbors, and their children were along creating a small caravan. They would all stay with various friends and family in Lochlan for three nights.

The two-hour wagon ride was long, but Jackson didn't care. Pa loaded a handmade bucket filled with fresh water covered with a wooden lid. A ladle hung from the rope handle. Lunch was a picnic of bread, fruit, cheese, and a scoop from the bucket.

The day was beautiful, with a sky as blue as Jack had ever seen. Farmland near Lochlan was alive with workers tending to crops. The sights were a welcome change from the sameness of Waddyshire. An occasional stop so Bridget could stretch her cramped legs and Oliver could rest the horses, was a welcome opportunity for Jackson and Dutch to play fetch.

On a farm road on the outskirts of Lochlan 's Westside, the Merriweather Lane Market began and continued until it wound past shops and businesses. Uncle Fredrick and Aunt Polly lived a few roads off Merriweather Lane, just a block from the city barn where Jackson would stable his horse. The chestnut-colored steed stood sixteen hands tall.

The winning purse would give his family extra money if Jackson won the race the following day at Craggy Crook Downs. They could pay the taxes on the cottage, the fields, and the blacksmith business for a whole year. Jackson was an excellent rider, but he had never entered an official competitive race before. This time, his family's financial security depended on Champion crossing the line first.

After a long visit and a light supper that evening, Jackson began to feel restless about the race the next morning. Craggy Crook Downs was a different type of race track than any the Jones family had seen. They were all anxious to see a lopsided track. Jack began to pace around the large house with twice the number of rooms as their cottage in Waddyshire.

Uncle Frederick had different advantages than Oliver. Frederick was able to finish school before their father died. When he got an excellent job at a bank, he and Aunt Polly moved to Lochlan. Their home was a three-story blue house attached to the next home, with many other houses in a row. Aunt Polly didn't cook in the gathering room over the fireplace like his mum. She enjoyed her real kitchen with its red brick floor.

After Aunt Polly cleared the supper dishes, Uncle Frederick fetched tea and sat back down at the dining table. "Jackson, you'd better come over here and listen to this,"

Frederick said. Aunt Polly brought a full teapot to the mahogany table as she and Bridget rejoined them.

"The track is called Craggy Crook," Frederick began to explain. "It got its name from the outer loop, bounded by a steep wall of rugged rocks. The *crook* is for the track's deep bend, creating a pear-shaped track, a challenge for any rider, not just around and around."

"You be careful on Champion, Jack," his mum cautioned. "Since neither the rider nor the horse has raced on a crooked track, you might not be ready. Local riders may have practiced for weeks."

"I don't know about that, Bridget," Polly drew out slowly. "They locked the gate at the track weeks ago, hoping to make the competition fair."

"If it were a steeplechase race, the riders would just practice jumping over those fences," Bridget agreed.

"Bridget, me love, I didn't know you knew that much about horse racing." Oliver's eyes grew large as he sipped his tea. "Steeplechase, is it?"

"Well," she announced as she placed her cup on its saucer, "if the Queen can love horse racing…so can I."

"Me too, Mummy," Jemima chimed in.

Bridget smiled. Turning to Jack, she added, "Mimee and I will set up our booth while you young men take Champion over to the racetrack. You two will have to spruce up your handsome mount a little when you get there. Jack, give him a good brushing to calm him down. I'm not sure if Becky will help her family or Mimee and me." Bridget sipped at her steaming brew. She took a bite of Polly's wonderful bread that remained on the table and swooned with enjoyment. "Jack, have another piece of bread. It is delicious."

Jackson picked up some bread with scattered focus as he watched his cousin, Carlton, bound down the steps, two at a time. "Becky said her mum and pa won't set up a large vendor booth. Since her mother was sick last winter, there won't be extra sales at the Market for them. Her pa will sell the shoes and boots he made. His cobbler's bench is the most detailed in the shire."

Carlton laughed and pointed at the horn. "Are you going to wear that pouch in the race, Jackson? You take that thing with you wherever you go? Is it made of pound sterling?"

"Silver?" Jackson laughed and glanced at his father. "No…not silver."

Jack," his father interrupted. "I'll keep your bag for you." Oliver reached for the bag and threw it over his shoulder. "No, Carlton. It's a horn. Jack is a smashing hornblower. He keeps it nearby so he can practice anytime."

Jackson grinned. Well, it was true. It wasn't pound sterling.

· · · · ·

In the morning, when the tall clock in the front hall chimed seven AM, Jackson and Carlton darted out the front door and walked down to the neighborhood barn. It was a beautiful morning. The air smelled clean, and birds sang from branches high in the trees.

"How many riders have entered the race?" Jackson asked as they neared the livery stable.

Entering the barn, Carlton waved at Godfrey, the stable hand. "Mornin' Mate." Carlton stopped a second. "Um, you make the ninth rider, Jack." The cousins found Champion in the third stall.

The two boys saddled the tall mount and swung up onto his back. Jack's feet were in the stirrups, and Carlton hung on from behind. It was only a mile to the track. Aunt Polly and Uncle Fredrick would share their large surrey with Jackson's family and meet the boys later at the racetrack.

Chapter Sixteen

Craggy Crook Downs

The grandstands at Craggy Crook Downs were already filling when the rest of the Jones family arrived. People from Lochlan cheered on local favorites as grooms led the horses into the paddock where their trainer saddled them. Since Jackson was the owner, trainer, and jockey, he prepared Champion for the entry parade around the warm-up area. Unable to afford a suit of jockey colors or racing silks, Jackson tied a light blue scarf around his neck.

The Downs were magnificent, unlike any the Jones family had seen. Jackson often raced other riders in the field beyond the village at home. But Craggy Crook Downs was nothing like that. The race track, packed and raked until the dirt was free of anything that would trip a racehorse or twist a valuable animal's ankle, shone like the track at Royal Ascot.

The visitors' observation area wasn't a spot on the grass where families could spread a blanket and enjoy a sandwich while waiting for the race to begin. The stands were four tiers high, framed with sturdy Scots pine lumber, with the same pine planks laid, end-for-end, for seating. It was a fancy new type of construction, none that Waddyshire had seen.

The Jones family's excitement mounted as the time for the race neared. "Mummy," Jemima wrung her hands together, "when will the race start?"

"Any minute, Honey," Bridget said as she smoothed her skirt for the tenth time.

Dutch wiggled and watched all the proceedings. The dog was Champion's stable-mate. Dutch didn't want to be far from the horse's side at the racetrack. Inside the track, once the horses and riders were due at the starting point, Oliver had the dog on a leash to not frighten the other horses or make them skittish.

"Riders up," the paddock judge called above the noise of the racing enthusiasts.

With that one instruction, each jockey got a leg up from their trainer, or in Jackson's case, from his cousin Carlton. The gate crew guided the horses and riders behind the scratch line and waited for the starter to blow the whistle.

Excited and ready to run, Champion pranced inside the small starting area. Then, everything seemed to grow silent. The shrill sound of the whistle split the air, and the horses burst forth from the gates as the crowd roared.

Champion charged out like a true frontrunner, setting the pace for the entire pack. The track was more than a mile long. Divided into furlongs, or eighth-mile lengths, Craggy Crook was over eight furlongs. A white pole, painted in different colors, marked the course at each furlong.

"They're passing the black-and-white pole," Frederick yelled as the horses passed the first sixteenth mile. "A half a furlong."

"Oh, Pa," Jemima squealed, "I can't stand to watch."

"Cover your eyes, Mimee," her mother cautioned, putting her arm around the girl without taking her eyes off the track.

The flying horses and expert riders pounded around the green-and-white pole, just one furlong from the end. The important distance pole stood at the finish line. Who would cross the wire first and end up in the winner's circle?

Even the runner-up purse, the *place* position, would help the Jones family. But the *first*-place earnings would secure them for the next year. Jackson's family leaped to their feet as the first three horses came into the homestretch. The roar of the crowd was deafening.

The third-place horse, in *show* position, began to slow in his stride. The jockey leaned into the saddle even further, but the horse's pace only slackened more. When the final two horses crossed the finish line, Champion came in first. Jack won the Derby by three lengths.

Oliver, Bridget, Jemima, and the rest of the family spilled out of the stands and ran to the finish line. Jackson paraded Champion in front of the cheering crowd. Some horse-racing fans were waving their hands; others raced to pick up their winnings. In their large, flowered hats with huge plumes, even little ladies hurried out of the stands. They tried to get to the front of the line at the payout window.

Jackson's family joined the track officials in the winner's circle. Oliver wore his Sunday suit, with the leather pouch across his shoulder. Bridget chose her best dress and blue hat. Jack remained on Champion's back as a track official placed a wreath of flowers around the horse's neck.

Armstrong Hughes, the famous quick-drawing sketcher, stood with his art pad tucked into the crook of his arm. The artist rapidly drew a picture of Jackson on Champion's back, with his parents and sister standing beside him. Carlton watched over the artist's shoulder as a marvelous likeness of Jackson appeared on the paper. Jackie saw Becky jumping up and down on the sidelines, laughing and smiling so much it looked like her cheeks would hurt.

The Jones family had no stable hands to act as hot-walkers. Jack cared for Champion, trained him, and rode him into the winner's circle. After the ceremonial formalities, he dismounted and walked the horse to cool him down. Jack did it all, owner, trainer, groom, jockey, and hot-walker. This time, Dutch was along to walk with his friend.

"Craggy Crook Downs announces the winner of the largest purse of the Derby. Jackson Jones won with the fastest-paced racehorse in the history of the track. A winning check was issued and presented to Jack." By noon, the area newspaper would print the story. Below the caption, the paper would include the sketch Armstrong Hughes had done of the winner, Jackson Jones, and his family.

Is that what the deer meant? Am I the one to save my family from financial ruin? Jackson wondered.

Chapter Seventeen

The Market Road in Lochlan

Merriweather Lane Market and Fair ran from Tricky Tavy's Travel Treasures to the store farthest from town, Ichatha Fisher's Fresh Fishery. That location was a true blessing, considering it kept the odor of the fish market as far from the vendors as possible.

The Lachlan Fair was larger than the family remembered. Maybe they thought that every year. Still, the capital city was growing, and so was the fabulous fair. The city swarmed with people from near and far.

In the summer months, fruit and vegetable markets offered more food than usual. Cookie and bread vendors competed with people who usually sold baked goods on Market Day. That was fine with Jemima. She could buy as many cookies as her mother would allow.

The aroma of yeasty bread and biscuits from the bakery, and the sweet perfume of flowers from a nearby stand, blocked the usual unfriendly smell of the exciting city. Normally, fireplace smoke from breakfast preparation hung like a morning fog over Lochlan at any time of year. Horse droppings that lay in the street until trampled by the next carriage added to the unpleasant aroma. Lochlan didn't smell like the fresh air of the rolling grassland at home. Still, a squirt in a handkerchief from a small bottle of lavender cologne could chase away most unwanted odors.

Situated outside the Lochlan Bank building, the fair booth where the Jones family sold their goods was in a good location. People could go to the bank and draw out more money for the handmade goods once they spent their first allowance.

A woman with a bindi, or red dot, on her forehead walked past them. Jemima knew that meant the woman was probably from India and was married. The man with her wore a familiar white suit and white hat. Jemima watched as they walked into an Indian Import store a few doors past.

The streets bustled with people. Men and women with lilting Scottish voices and tartan plaid accenting their clothing mingled with a family chattering in a language Jemima didn't understand. There were people from many cultures, men in long beards and some in French berets. Some people had dark skin; some had light; some had freckles; some had none. Everyone enjoyed the many craft and trade booths of the thriving market. Most people wore their church clothes that morning, which were not nearly as fancy as the attire of the wealthy.

The booth Oliver set up consisted of two large oak barrels he bought from a cooper in Lochlan two years before and stored in Frederick's basement. With one of the barrels at each end, Oliver placed wide plank boards between them to create a huge table for all their merchandise. Then Bridget and Jemima covered all the beautifully crafted items they placed on the table with clean cloths. Oliver hired two young boys to guard the booth and the Hampton's table next to it while the family and friends were at the horse race.

Following the race, while Jackson and Carlton rode Champion back to the stable, Bridget pulled the old pieces of fabric back from the merchandise. News of the race had spread. The guard boys eagerly shook Bridget's hand as the mother of the newest hero in Lochlan.

It was a beautiful sunny day. Jemima ran across the street to the Buns and Butternut Bread Bakery and brought back some food to nibble on. She and her mum had little time for eating as their customers eagerly inspected their merchandise.

Rebecca Hampton and her family were at the table beside them. Becky was making a sale of fancy shoelaces she knitted with tight threads of fine string when a younger boy than she stopped and watched. The laces were red and black and would make a fine addition to any outfit if one were to have a playful nature.

"May I help you find something?" Becky asked the boy. She liked children and often helped the primary school teacher with younger students who needed tutoring. She had a way of encouraging young ones in her care.

"Do you know the smithy with that little anvil at the next table?" The boy's eyes were large and hopeful.

"Yes, I do." Becky started to put both hands on her hips and then remembered. Friends told her that her hands-on-hips posture made her look like a strict schoolmarm. She smiled and slipped her hands into the pockets of the pinafore she wore over her dress. "The blacksmith is back by his carriage."

"Thanks, Missy." The youngster tipped his cap as he walked around the side of the bank building where some vendors had parked their wagons or buggies. "Good afternoon, Mister," the young boy greeted Oliver. "Got a situation here." He handed him a tin cup with a distinct dent in the side.

"So, I see," Oliver said with a smile.

"It's my fault," the ten-year-old said with his head hung low. "I accidentally sat on it." He looked up with pleading eyes, "You have a lot of stuff here that you made. Can you fix my pa's cup?"

A tall thin man with a top hat and a morning coat over a double-breasted vest looked at the metal cup's dint. "Why don't you buy a new one, young man?"

"A new one?" the boy questioned with a frown. "This one is my pa's."

"Very caring of you." To Oliver, top-hat-man asked, "Can you fix the cup?"

"Come over here," Oliver offered. Together, Oliver and the boy walked around the family buggy. Behind the seats, under a tattered old quilt, Oliver reached for a small anvil and a smoothly warn wooden hammer.

"Can ya fix it, Mister?" the boy asked.

Oliver inspected it and said, "Of course, I can. Let's have a go with it," he encouraged as he smiled at the boy. "What's your name?"

"Ambrose," the boy said with a sniff.

The man in the fancy coat added, "My name is Fastidious Fog. I own a bookstore in Lochlan, not far from here." Fog addressed Ambrose, "Young man, I am glad you are careful with your money. If the cup is still good, fix it."

Ambrose smiled. "It's my pa's cup," he repeated.

Oliver put Bridget's old darning egg into Ambrose's cup and said to the boy, "The wooden ball on the stick looks like a lollypop egg, doesn't it?"

Ambrose held his breath and remained silent.

Holding the wooden mallet securely, Oliver used his other hand to balance the cup on top of the anvil. As carefully as if it were a silver goblet for a king, Oliver lightly pounded the dent out of the cup. Before the child's eyes, Oliver reshaped the cup with the help of the egg and smoothed the surface with the mallet.

The breath burst from Ambrose's lips as he finally exhaled. "You did it," he squealed.

Oliver held the cup up to the sunlight, turning it around and around. "Yes, I believe I did."

"How much do I owe you, Mister?" With squinting eyes, Ambrose waited for an amount. He probably couldn't pay for the fine artful work anyway.

"Two-pence will do it."

Ambrose reached into his pocket and took out one copper. Holding it up, he breathed deeply. "I just have one, Mister."

"Well, now, isn't that a coincidence?" Putting his hand in his vest pocket, Oliver found one brown coin. "I have a piece, too. I'll add this one to yours." He took the coin and slipped it into his pocket. "A man pays his bills, son. Today, you are a man."

Bridget, who had come around the bank building looking for Oliver, gave her husband a sideways hug. "You're a good man, Oliver Jones."

As Ambrose bounded away with his father's cup held tightly between both hands, Mr. Fog patted Oliver on the back. "I agree. You're a good man." He reached in his vest pocket and pulled out a sixpence. He turned Oliver's hand up and pressed the coin in the smithy's palm. Mr. Fog took off his hat, revealing dry straight gray hair. He bowed slightly, then put his hat back on. With that, **Fastidious** Fog twirled his walking stick in the air and moved on to enjoy the handmade wares of several booths down the way.

Chapter Seventeen

After the Race

After the race at Craggy Crook Downs, Jackson, and Carlton rode Champion back to the city stable. Jack was still flying high with the thrill of coming in first.

In the stable, Jackson grabbed the brushes from the leather pouch they were stored in and began giving Champion a rub down. He placed his cheek on the side of the horse's face and sighed. "You were great, boy."

Carlton reached for the brush. "Jackson, if you want to rejoin your family, I'd be happy to brush her out and walk her around."

Jackson's smile was even wider. "That would be great." He grabbed an old towel from the pouch and wiped from his face the mud the other horses kicked. To his thinking, he was ready for the fair. Jackson tore out of the barn and ran back to join the family.

Jack thought about Champion and the flowers around the horse's neck. And he remembered his winnings. Jack's hands trembled when the track official handed him the money. A fixed amount would excite any young jockey. That morning, however, Jack received more than he planned. He got the winner's purse, plus one percent of all the money the track took in that day, as the jockey's earnings. They handed Jack enough money to pay the bills as planned, plus much more. Jack would pick up one last prize, a trophy with a mounted horse and rider on top. An experienced engraver and store owner on Merriweather Lane would expertly inscribe Jack's name across the marble base. Jackson was a winner.

Chapter Eighteen

A Good Day's Work on a Good Day

Back at the table, Oliver kissed Bridget on the cheek. "How are your beautiful goods doing? I saw a lot of customers gathered around."

"It looks like a good day, Mum." Jackson beamed as he darted up to the table.

"It has been a good day, indeed," Bridget said with a smile.

Becky left her mother in charge of their booth and joined Jackson in the excitement of a good sales day. "We have sold most of our things, too."

Bridget gave Becky a sideways hug. "That is wonderful, Rebecca. We'll be sold out here in a short while," Bridget said as she rubbed her palms together eagerly. "People from last year and the year before looked for us. Jemima put a sign on the table when she set up, so they were waiting for us when we got back from the racetrack."

Becky watched as a familiar man came up to the table. His clothes were clean but worn. Even his fingernails were clean. Still, there was something that made Becky cringe. She wrapped her arms around her body to fight off the trembling caused by standing too close to the gravedigger.

"It is a bonny day, Miss Hampton." The trampish man with decaying teeth tipped his hat. "You look lovely, Becky."

"Digger?" Jackson asked. "I hardly recognized you."

Bridget smiled, "It looks like you cleaned up for your day in Lochlan, Digger. New clothes?"

"The Vicar gave me a fresh set of clothes," Jinx answered and pointed on down the lane. "More booths to enjoy. I want to see as many vendors as I can before I get back to me table. Me water-reed dolls are selling smashing fine," he said. "Oh, and Mrs. Pierpont gave me the round, straight sticks from her downed birch tree. With bundles of heather I collected, I made besoms. They are nice brooms, fine twigs held together with twine the Vicar saved from newspaper bundles. The paper comes into the store next door to the church." Digger smiled with pride. "I have the besoms for sale, too."

A lady with a white bonnet tied under her chin hurried up to the booth as Digger moved on. "Mrs. Jones, I am so glad your booth is still open."

"Mrs. Honeywell, isn't it?" Bridget clasped the hand of the middle-aged woman. "I remember you from last year. Are you alright?" To Jackson, she said, "Jack, pull my stool around here for Mrs. Honeywell."

"Happy to," Jack said. The wooden stool was a special one. His pa designed it and made it himself. The legs folded under for ease in carrying and storing.

"Thank you," Mrs. Honeywell said as she sat down on the white-painted seat. She looked past her full skirt and down at the legs of the little chair on which she sat. "Where did you get such a wonderful stool?"

"My husband designed the chair and made it himself. We brought a few with us." Bridget pointed to the wooden folding stools and then at her husband. "This is Oliver."

Mrs. Honeywell reached out her hand. "So happy to meet you. I came to buy some more of your wonderful large spoons and doilies for the back of my new settee. Also, I need four buttons for the coat I am making for my daughter, and now, a stool." She was embarrassed and smiled a little. "I will use the stool to keep nearby. I am expecting my fifth child. I tire easily."

"Mrs. Honeywell, that is wonderful," Bridget said, smiling.

"Please, call me, Moyra, Mrs. Jones." She looked again at the bare table. "I was hoping you might have some booties and sweaters for wee ones. The other children are old enough that I already gave away their baby things to my friends."

Bridget threw a hand to her mouth in surprise. "I'm Bridget, Moyra. I would love to crochet some baby things for your little one. Make a list of what you need. We will see Oliver's brother and his family at Christmas time. I could bring them to you then."

"Perfect," Moyra Honeywell exclaimed as she reached in her purse. "I am so pleased. Here is payment for my buttons and the other things for today." Then she pulled out another bill from a small coin purse. "Here is a quid for thread or yarn and a down payment on the clothes. Since we don't know if the baby will be a boy or girl, you can make them in white and some items in pale green."

"A whole pound, Moyra? That is too much money," Bridget protested.

"Nonsense." Moyra took Bridget's hand in hers. "I'll bring a list over to you tomorrow if you will still be in town. We live across the street from your brother and his family. I saw them stop at your booth and visit a little while today."

Bridget got out a cloth, draw-string bag. "That will be fine. You pick out your spoons, doilies, and buttons. Jack will help you carry the stool home."

"I'll help, too," Becky offered.

Oliver raised both hands. "You are both a blessing. Thank you."

Moyra Honeywell picked out the items she bought and put them in the bag. She also selected four large spoons from the few Bridget had left. Jack took the folding stool, and Becky carried the shopping bag. They also gathered up the other packages Moyra purchased from other street vendors. Together, they walked with Mrs. Honeywell a few streets over.

"Bridget, our booth sales were smashing," Oliver whispered to not bother others with their business. "Add the booth money to the prize winnings, and we should have a whopping good amount to hold us over next winter. We could give Jack a little money. He won the purse. And, you may be able to buy some yard goods in the village to make yourself a new dress."

"Oh no," she protested. "Jemima is growing. She needs a new dress more than I." Bridget was not one to think of herself first.

"I can save you some money by making the buttons. So, you may be able to buy enough goods to make a bodice and skirt for each of you. Jemima can sew now. She can make her own."

Bridget looked at the Hampton family's table. Their booth was also empty. Given that they had fewer items to sell, they had done well. Polly and Frederick had shopped rather than sold. It was a perfect day to spend at the market. It was time to go home for Jackson's celebration feast.

Chapter Nineteen

The Trophy

Later, back at the house, Aunt Polly answered a knock on the door and invited Becky in. "My dear, welcome."

"Hi, Becky," Jack bubbled as he bounded in from the backyard. "Come in a minute." He pointed to the settee in the parlor. "We're all going down to pick up the trophy in a flash." He blushed a little as he watched his soaked clothes drip on Aunt Polly's carpet. "I washed by up-turning the bucket under the hand pump in the back yard on myself. Gotta run upstairs and get out of these wet clothes."

"I am so proud of you, Jackie." Becky oozed excitement and gave him a jolly hug, careful not to get her clothes wet from his.

Jack quickly glanced at Carlton for his reaction. "Thanks, Becky," Jackson blushed. "Are your parents going?"

"They are for sure," she said as she giggled and grabbed his arm.

"Hurry up and get into dry clothes, me-laddie," Oliver sparkled. "Let's get going."

Jackson bounded up the steps two at a time. The sound of banging doors and slamming drawers filled the house. As quickly as he ran up the stairs, he soon darted back down.

"Here, I'll trade you, Pa." Jack reached in his jacket pocket and pulled out the large brown envelope with his winnings. "You take this, and I'll take the pouch."

"Will we have lunch when we get back, dear?" Bridget asked as she patted Polly on the shoulder.

"I'll cook up something," Aunt Polly said and chuckled.

"Becky," Polly took her bonnet off the hall tree and tied the straw hat around her neck. "You and your parents can come to eat, too."

"Thank you. But we walked over to Crabtree's Fish and Chips Restaurant," she swooned. "It was scrumptious."

"That sounds tremendous," Jemima squealed. Dutch crept over and sniffed around at Becky's skirt hem. "Dutch smells the fish and approves of your choice," Jemima said with a laugh.

Jack linked his arm into Becky's, and together they pushed Carlton out the door. The Hamptons met them at the end of the sidewalk, and they all walked over to Merriweather Lane.

All along the path to the Market, Dutch led the way on the front end of the leash. It was a boomer day, with the bluest sky and clearest air. When they got to the store, Jack wrapped Dutch's leash around his hand and went inside.

"Welcome to Phineas Boggs' Froggy Bottom Unique Gifts, and your little dog, too," a woman with dark curls piled high on her head offered as they entered. "What can I do for you?"

"Well," Jackson stammered. "I ah…"

"I know who he is," Fastidious Fog offered with a smile as he moved from the other side of the store.

"Oh, my Uncle Morty! I know who you are, too." The woman put her fingertips to her lips in amazement. "You are him," she gasped as she pointed to a stack of newspapers. There, on page one, was the sketch Armstrong Hughes drew at the racetrack. Even though mud splattered his face, Jackson's wide grin beamed from the Westside Gazette.

Mr. Fog stepped in again, "Jackson Jones, the fastest man on a horse."

"Yes, he is." A man in a black bowler hat and a three-piece pinstriped suit agreed.

"Who are you, Sir?" Oliver Jones questioned. "I don't think I like the notoriety this race has caused our family."

Jackson, Becky, and Carlton grew quiet. Who was this man who approached them?

"Should we leave, Jackie?" Becky asked and then looked at her mother and father, standing with Bridget.

Charlie Hampton's eyes flashed as he measured the stranger from head to foot. "No, Rebecca. You stay here in the store with the rest of us."

Jack immediately recognized the concerns. He knew that his father carried the race winnings in his inside jacket pocket. More than aware that a valuable golden horn hung from his shoulder, Jackson wondered if they had come out into public too soon following the race. A crowd could be bold enough to attack, or a small gathering of people could discourage someone who wished to harm them. As other shoppers crowded into the little shop, Jack thought, *Is this a good thing or a bad thing?*

The man removed his hat and placed it across his chest. "I understand. May I explain? I am a solicitor, Alexander Curmudgeon," he announced. "I handle many of William Fairmont, the Earl of Mooreland's, legal matters."

"The earl?" Bridget gulped. "His home is miles from Waddyshire—in the hills."

"Yes, Ma'am." Mr. Curmudgeon bowed slightly. "The Master of the King's Horses told the earl's head stablemaster, you would come here to Froggy Bottom's to pick up your winner's cup. Phineas Boggs would have it engraved by now."

"And, here it is," Mr. Boggs announced as he handed Jackson the foot-tall winner's trophy.

The new celebrity jockey reached for the trophy and cradled it carefully in his arms. "Thank you, Mr. Boggs."

"Thank you for winning, Mr. Jones." Phineas patted the boy's shoulder. "I won a good purse of my own from your expert riding. You have a fast horse."

"Thanks again." Jackson bowed a bit from the hips.

"Do you know this man?" Oliver asked the proprietor as he pointed to Alexander Curmudgeon.

"Yes, of course. Everyone knows Mr. Curmudgeon."

"Good," The tension in Oliver's shoulders relaxed as he studied the man further.

"I thank you for the testimonial regarding my identity," the earl's attorney said with a slight bow. "Jackson, His Lordship loves horses and dogs," he added, motioning to Dutch. "He asked me to invite you, your family, and your dog to have dinner with him and the countess this evening at seven PM. Can he expect you?"

Jackson looked at the attorney with wide eyes. Still, he said nothing.

"When you arrive at the castle, I have special instructions. As you may know from tabloid accounts, there have been a few attempts on His Lordship's life."

Bridget gasped. "I read about a man who fired two shots at the earl's carriage while riding in Lochlan. That was about ten years ago."

Mr. Curmudgeon added. "Yes, Ma'am. It happened in 1842 and again last year. Some months ago, a man hit the earl in the head right there in the castle. The guards have always been careful about letting anyone get close to the earl or his home. They refuse to let it happen again." He reached in his pocket. "These are special two-pence coins," he said as he opened his palm, revealing a handful of small shiny copper coins about an inch wide. "The King saw the need for special identification in many of the homes in Arie. Each coin has the King's image on the front and his Palace on the back. Any visitor needs one of these at every estate in the country. I'll give one to each of you. And Jackson, there is one for Dutch, too."

The family laughed. Jack nuzzled the dog behind his ears.

Curmudgeon began again. "You must show these coins to the butler to enter the castle. Once inside the castle, you must surrender the coin, and the guard will replace it with a normal coin of the realm." He smiled as he passed out the coppers. "We want everyone to be safe."

"All these rules because Jack won the race?" Jemima laughed in amazement.

Mr. Curmudgeon smiled. "Winning the race is the special accomplishment that brought your brother to the earl's attention. Now, he is anxious to meet all of you after getting word from the master of his horses."

Jackson turned the coin over and over in his hand. "What word did his master pass along?"

Curmudgeon opened his mouth like he was going to correct Jackson. Smiling, he said quietly, "The earl has no master." Then, he swallowed hard and began again. "The word came through Mr. Barker, a fine man, and the Master of the King's Horses. He said he talked to hunters in Waddyshire, and they told Barker about the silencing of the Shaman. Barker passed the information to the earl's stablemaster." He asked Jack, "Do you know anything about that?"

"Me?" Jackson gulped so hard he nearly choked.

"We all know about the Shaman," Becky admitted. "The people in Waddyshire were freezing. Everything was turning to ice."

"We heard about that in Lochlan," Carlton chimed in.

Curmudgeon's eyes began to twinkle. "The earl's stableman said Barker talked with deer hunters in your area." He smiled a knowing smile.

"Oh, that is rich," Jackson said, trying hard to sound innocent of any connection to the events surrounding the Shaman-fey. "What did they know about it?"

"He reported, someone blew a horn in the evening hours in or beyond the shire." Alexander slipped into the tale of the Shaman and the music of the horn. "It lifted the villagers' spirits and quieted their fears."

"It did indeed," Becky added, pretending to know little about it. "No one knew who the horn player was, but his or her music was amazing."

"I was usually asleep before the music began." Jemima folded her arms as someone left out of the fun.

"You wouldn't be sad that you missed the sound of the horn that last night," Bridget teased her daughter.

Rebecca knew the night Jackie's mum was talking about very well. Becky had been there. But she also knew that Jackie's music and the horn were all still a secret. "That one awful night, just before the Shaman stopped blowing icy wind down into the valley, the music sounded like a dirge. It was a message of dread, painful memories, and lost hope."

"Everyone in the village heard it." Bridget held her stomach as thoughts of the music nearly doubled her over.

"People became sick," Oliver offered cautiously as he tried not to reveal too much. "Everyone except the young children who went to bed early and the old ones who had lost most of their hearing." He gave Jack a wink.

"I hope the musical laments didn't hurt anyone." Jackson's expression fell as guilt flooded over him.

"No, not at all," Oliver offered quickly before Jack's good heart flooded with grief. "It was like removing a sliver in the finger with a sharp needle. The painful pinprick was necessary to release the tiny chip of wood." He patted Jackson on the arm. "If the hornblower had not stopped the Shaman, many would have died from frost during the night."

"It was strange." Jack looked from his father to the solicitor. "The beautiful melodies soothed neighbors and others in the village. But it gave the Shaman-fey strength to do harm and reason to be evil. When the music changed, my friends and family became violently ill; but the Shaman lost all desire to harm others. The village thawed by morning, and the Shaman was gone.”

“You said, ‘my friends and family became ill.’ Didn’t you get sick?” Again, Mr. Curmudgeon’s eyes shone mischievously. He seemed to want to lead Jackson right up to a sacred secret and leave him room to wiggle his way out.

“Like my father said, ‘everyone got sick.’” Jack gulped and began again. “Did you say you invited us all for dinner tonight with the Earl of Mooreland?”

“Yes, I did,” Alexander agreed. “You, your parents, and your sister come to the castle early, about 6:30, so His Lordship doesn’t have to wait. He likes to eat on time.” Curmudgeon bowed slightly at Becky. “Your lady friend, Miss Hampton, is also welcome. And, don’t forget your dog. Countess Virginia will enjoy meeting him, too. She loves dogs. It is Dutch—right?”

“Yes, Sir,” Jackson said as the breath escaped from his lungs.

“Dinner with the Earl and Countess of Mooreland?” Becky squealed. “What do I wear to sup with the royals?”

“We’ll find something,” her mother said as she patted Becky on her back.

“As you dine with the **Earl of Moorland and Countess Virginia**,” Curmudgeon explained, “Dutch will join His Lordship’s dogs in the kitchen and feast on deer meat.” Curmudgeon reached down and nuzzled the dog behind his ears. “The earl won’t care what the dog is wearing,” he laughed.

Deer meat? Jackson's thoughts swam around in his head like minnows chased by a shark. Dutch’s food bowl never contained something as elegant as deer meet. As everyone chattered about the dinner invitation with the earl and his family, Jack's mind was elsewhere. Big Red’s pronouncement boomed in his head. He thought about what the deer hunters knew about Jack being *the one*. Memories of the evil Shaman and the magical music of the golden horn flooded in and nearly drowned him.

Chapter Twenty

A Visit to the Castle

Broadmoor Castle was five miles northwest of Lacklan. When they arrived, Oliver waited for the guards to open the iron gates at the entrance. Two men, dressed in red and black uniforms, checked the fancy invitation Mr. Curmudgeon had provided. One guard nodded, and Oliver drove Frederick's four-passenger surrey through the high, fancy entrance. Oliver and Bridget decided the family wagon they took to Lochlan would not be proper for dinner at a castle. They moved on through the entry arches into the large, brick-covered semi-circle that formed the courtyard. Oliver slow-walked the horse until the sorrel beauty stopped at the front door.

"This is it," Oliver said as he inhaled deeply.

"Bodacious!" Jackson's eyes swelled to the size of wagon wheels as he took in the earl's guards standing at attention on both sides of the front door.

"I like their tall black hats," Becky whispered. "They're so fluffy."

"That's bearskin, dear," Bridget explained. "Just like the guards at the King's palace."

"Bearskin?" Jackson asked with widened eyes. "From real bear?"

Oliver watched as the guard searched under and around the surrey. Then he whispered to Jackson. "The bear pelts come from Canada, Jack."

Knowing her squirmy daughter, Bridget leaned over and tapped Jemima on the shoulder. "Those hats are eighteen inches tall and weigh a pound and a half. Can you imagine standing with your body stiff and straight for two-hour shifts with that monstrosity on your head? I read that the earl thought if his guards looked like the King's sentries, people would be afraid to break in."

Jack was amazed by how well the guards stood at attention, with their straight as an arrow stance in fancy blue tunics. The jackets had a darker blue collar, shoulder stripes edged in white, and dark blue and white cuffs. Their uniform also consisted of black trousers with a white stripe down each seam. Their white leather buff belt held it all in place.

Bridget squinted as she looked carefully at the guard when the surrey stopped. "Oliver, do you think the fellow's gold buttons with the earl's insignia are some that you made?"

"It's improbable but possibly probable," Oliver said with a grin.

"What does that mean?" Jemima questioned as she wrinkled her nose in confusion.

Oliver reigned in the horse and turned to Jemima. "I don't know where the buttons I make end up. Dressmakers and tailor shops purchase the buttons. I suppose they could decorate a guardsman's tunic. The last order I filled did have the earl's insignia on them. I guess it is possible. But it seems strange to think my little buttons could do such an important job."

"Crikey!" Jemima sighed.

Looking at the huge building, Jackson gulped. *What is behind that massive door?*

Oliver shook his head in disbelief. "Dear," he called out in fun, "we're home."

"I wouldn't want to make curtains for all of those windows," Bridget sighed as she looked up at the massive castle.

"Wonder where they keep the chickens?" Jack cracked wise.

When the castle door opened, a carriage driver came to the surrey. He slipped onto the seat and took the reins.

"Why does the building sparkle?" Jemima asked as she looked high up the three stories.

The stable hand turned to her, "Miss, the building stones have specks of ancient fossils in them. That's what makes them twinkle in the light."

"Crikey," Jemima sighed in a whisper.

As Jackson, Becky, and the rest of the family got out and approached the entrance, an elegant butler opened one side of the huge door and announced, "Good evening."

"Good evening," they all mumbled back, eager to be there but unaware of what they should say or how they should act.

The butler held out a fancy, metal bank toward them. It looked heavy. Shaped like the front door to the castle, it was special. "Please, show me your entry coin and insert it into the slot on the top. Young Jackson, Dutch's coin as well."

They presented their two-pence copper to the butler, who carefully inspected it. Every coin made a deep mellow sound as it plunked to the bottom of the bank.

"Remember to curtsey, Jemima," Bridget reminded her. "Oh, my dear, dear me," Bridget moaned after a second. "I should be able to get down to curtsey, but I don't know how I'll get back up."

"You'll be fine, Bridge-love," Oliver whispered and smiled.

Jackson took his first steps into the massive castle and looked around at the grand entrance. Dutch walked at his heal, unafraid, prancing proudly. "Do we curtsey, too?" Jackson laughed nervously.

The butler said nothing but smiled a little.

"No," Oliver lowered his voice and tried to stifle a grin. "Women curtsey, Son, gentlemen bow. Just a slight bend at the waist."

"I am Abernathy, the butler. Come, follow me," the man instructed.

Jackson and his family walked through the grand entrance that opened into a gigantic marble reception hall. There were marble columns, marble steps off to the right, and marble everywhere. A royal blue carpet stretched out the length of the hall beneath an ornate tray ceiling with sparkling crystal chandeliers.

"The earl and countess will greet you in the Cozy Salon," the butler announced as Jackson's family came to the room in front of them off the hall. "It is a very comfortable room, colorful and inviting. May I take your bag, young Jackson?"

"No, thank you," Jack said as he clutched the horn more tightly. "I'll keep it with me."

Jemima asked, "The Cozy Salon?"

"Yes, Miss," the butler said and smiled. "The Golden Salon is much larger. The Cozy is very comfortable and perfect for greeting many guests. The Cozy Salon is where the family gathers to read the latest story to the children, have a pleasant conversation, and play board games."

"Like our gathering room is a cuddle space," Jemima said as she nodded.

The butler led them past the gloriously ornate Golden Salon, with its two white and gold-trimmed couches facing each other. Side chairs provided light blue accents, making the white marble fireplace dazzle. Pictures, mostly of what looked like the earl's ancestors, hung from the walls creating the look of an art gallery. Jackson slowed and took in the familiar landscape paintings of the heath with flowering violet heather and the mountains near Waddyshire.

Jackson saw the facing couches in the sitting area near the fireplace. He wanted to run his hand over the thick, lustrous surface and shine of the couch fabric. Jack thought he had stepped into a fairytale.

Chapter Twenty-One

Lady Grace Leads the Way

"My lady," Abernathy said with a fun smile when a young girl in a fancy white dress walked in. Turning to the visitors, he said, "May I present, Lady Grace, the earl's eldest daughter."

The nine-year-old proper little lady entered the room gracefully. Dressed in white lace from hairbow to stockings with a light blue ribbon-sash around her waist, she reached out her hand to the guests. Jackson's excitement began to settle. The elegant lady-in-training, Lady Grace, had a way of making people relax.

Lady Grace smiled and said, "Bonjour, heureux de vous rencontrer."

"And bonjour to you," Jackson answered but did not admit that "hello' was the only word in French he knew.

The little lady added, "Nous appelons, Thomas, Tommy."

Abernathy looked at Lady Grace with a warry eye. "She said, 'We call Lord Thomas, Tommy.' He will be in shortly."

"Thank you, Abernathy." Then Lady Grace turned to Jackson. "I am sorry for being rude." She smoothed her dress. Grace smiled and added, "Papa says it isn't polite to talk in a language that guests do not speak. I am so happy to meet the Craggy Crook Downs Derby winner."

Jackson looked at Abernathy, nodding slightly, then bowed a little. "I'm glad to meet you too, Lady Grace."

Abernathy introduced, "These young ladies are Rebecca Hampton and young Jones' sister, Jemima. The adults are Jackson's parents, Mr. and Mrs. Jones."

Grace smiled and brushed back her hair. "I am very pleased to meet you all. Mama said her hair has a mind of its own today. So, she's running a little late. But she told me I could show you the playroom if Abernathy comes with us."

"Of course, Ma'am." Turning to Oliver and Bridget, he added, "I'll be happy to show the children some rooms on this floor. You are welcome to come along, or you can wait here in the comfortable Cozy Room."

Bridget spoke up right away. "I would love to see the castle. But I'll let Jackson and Rebecca take the lead."

"Me too," Jemima joined in.

Jackson's mum gave Jemima a little hug. "Sorry, Mimee. You and Lady Grace are about the same age. I guess you should be upfront with everyone."

Grace smiled and started out showing them around like a tour guide. "The schoolroom is next door."

The School Room

The children's schoolroom was next to the Cozy Salon. Many people in the shire knew that Countess Virginia believed her children's education was important. She kept an eye, and an ear, on them while reading in the family's sitting room or painting in her art studio on the other side of the classroom.

Jackson followed Lady Grace into the classroom with Rebecca at his side. The room was large.

Lady Grace walked up to the chalkboard and picked up a piece of chalk. "Our teacher is here from eight until four in the afternoon. He isn't here on Saturdays." She folded her hands together and squared off her feet. "Boys and girls, quiet now," Grace said with a Scottish accent. "I am your new teacher, Dougal MacDougal. If you work hard, we will get along fine." She turned and wrote the teacher's name on the blackboard.

"Colored chalk." Jackson watched as she wrote, with large blue letters, across smaller slates, cobbled together and mounted to a large board. Jack's mouth dropped open.

Grace switched from her role as her teacher, back to her job as tour guide. "Mr. MacDougal's grandfather was James Pillans, the teacher who invented colored chalk. Mr. MacDougal told us his grandfather used ground chalk, dyes, and porridge to make it."

"Porridge?" Jemima wrinkled her face with questions. "Like oatmeal?"

Bridget patted Jemima's shoulder. "Like oatmeal or other grains."

Another blackboard hung on the other wall, with white and colored chalk sticks nearby. There was so much to see. Jackson was amazed. He wondered what it would have been like to go to school in such a well-furnished classroom. "You have a large globe of the world sitting right here in the room." In front of the window, a low bookcase holding books of many sizes, colors, and subjects caused Jack to swoon again.

The Playroom

Lady Grace bounced on her toes impatiently. "I'm anxious to show you the playroom."

Large, sliding pocket doors opened from the class into the playroom. Once inside, another sliding double-door opened into the hall. When the doors slid back, Jackson saw the room was no ordinary space of games and balls. It was a gymnasium.

"Crikey, look at that," Jackson whispered.

A broad, white strip ran along the far side of the room with ten carved, wooden soldiers at the end. Becky shook her head. "Looks like they brought Bowling-on-the-Green inside."

"It is," Lady Grace said as she ran over to the alley.

"Now it's Bowling-on-the-White," Jack said slowly. "It looks like they covered the floor with sheep's wool to make the wooden floor soft like the grass."

"You're right," Grace said with a giggle. "See the pins? Mama made them."

"She carved them to look like the King's soldiers?" Jackson was amazed.

Grace lowered her eyes and smiled. "Mummy said not to boast. But, she's an artist."

Becky pointed at two contraptions with wheels, "What are those?"

Jackson couldn't believe his eyes. "Two tricycles."

"Tri… what?"

"I read about them," Jackson admitted but could hardly believe what he saw. "But these are different. These two are shorter, small enough for you to ride, Lady Grace. Wonder who changed the design?"

"Papa designed them and had them built," Grace explained as she ran over to the tricycles.

"I heard the earl likes to invent things," Becky suggested.

The tricycles had two large back wheels, about twenty-four inches in diameter, and one wheel of the same size in the front. Each of the two tricycles had a seat with a sturdy back for balance, mounted on a frame. The earl attached two foot-pedals.

"It looks like a lot of fun," Jack said and smiled.

"Get on it," Grace offered Jackson. "You too, Miss Hampton."

"Rebecca, my Lady. Call me Rebecca," Becky said as she climbed on the high-wheeling tricycle. "Jackson," she squealed, "this is fun. We need these in Waddyshire. We could get around the village in a flash."

Jackson had so much fun he barely said anything. He could feel his smile take over his face.

"Look," Becky said as she pointed. "There's a balance beam, climbing ropes, and—"

"We work out here as part of our school work," Grace explained. "Mummy wants us to exercise. Once a week, we have dance lessons in the ballroom. Twice a week, we ride our ponies."

"Crikey, ponies?" Jemima gasped.

"We'd better go back to the salon," the butler reminded them.

"Alright," Grace agreed. "We'll just take a peek at Mummy's art studio."

The Art Studio

They stepped into Countess Virginia's art studio near the classroom on the way back to the Cozy Salon. Lady Grace whispered, "When Mummy paints, she wants to be near us as we work and play."

"Look at this," Becky whispered with a sigh. "The countess is quite a painter."

"Some of her paintings hang in the National Gallery," Abernathy said quietly.

An art easel stood in the middle of the room. A canvas covered with a white cloth waited for Lady Virginia to return. Another easel was near the window. The painting wasn't covered. Even though only half-done, Jack could see it would be beautiful. It looked like the rose bushes blooming in the garden beyond the windows.

The Dining Room

As they passed the formal dining room, everyone slowed to see the elegant space. The table, stretched to its fullest, had fourteen chairs on each side and one at each end, all slid into place underneath. Jackson stopped and tried to figure out the room. He didn't think he had enough relatives to fill thirty chairs.

The ceiling was high and beautifully decorated, like the others in the castle. Plaster cherubs reached out from each corner, connected by a golden ribbon around the room. Three sparkling cut-glass chandeliers hung low.

"Abernathy," Jackson observed, "you need no stepladder to light the ceiling candleholder."

The Golden Salon

They passed the Golden Salon, near the Broadmoor Staircase, when they first came in. Abernathy explained, "His Lordship uses the gilded room as a reception area when people in satin and lace come to a ball."

"It is beautiful," Bridgit whispered in awe.

Carved-frame armchairs with needlepoint upholstery lined the walls. "We arrange the chairs into conversation groupings when there is need," Abernathy described.

Music Room

The Music Room opened from the Golden Salon and the hall. Grace gestured to the seven-and-a-half-foot-long concert grand piano that sat in front of the massive windows. "We use the room after dinner most evenings. If we have guests, we set chairs in the Golden Salon and open the big folding doors between the two rooms."

A twenty-one-string, glossy white harp, accented with sprays of carved roses, sat beside the piano. "Do you play the harp?" Becky asked in amazement.

"I am learning," Lady Grace said with a sheepish smile.

"You are learning a lot," Jackson said in amazement.

Chapter Twenty-Two
A Very Special Meeting

Back in the Cozy Salon, Abernathy directed them to the couches and chairs. "Please sit down." He started to leave, then turned and added, "When the earl comes in, rise, and bow slightly, or curtsey a little to the countess. Don't sit down until His Lordship sits and tells you to do the same. You may refer to William Fairmont as the Earl of Mooreland, Lord Mooreland, His Lordship, His Grace, and other names handed down to him. If you are stuck, *Sir* will work."

Jackson wondered if he would remember all of the earl's names. Though his own name was Jackson, some called him Jack, and Becky called him Jackie. Jack thought it would take the classroom chalkboard to hold all of the earl's.

Jackson sat on the edge of a soft, light tan, leather-covered sofa. His leg muscles were tight, and his knees bounced rapidly like many young men his age. Wringing his hands together, he reached over and patted Becky's fingers.

Becky was so quiet Jackson couldn't figure it out. Was it because Becky was overwhelmed with all the amazing things she saw?

"Jack, sit still, please," his mother cautioned him. "You're making me nervous. Your leg is pumping as fast as mine when I work the treadle on my sewing machine."

"Yes, ma'am." But inside, Jackson felt jitters crawling around in his legs. It felt like a dozen mice were creeping along the walls of his skin. He had to admit, after touring the first floor of the castle with Lady Grace, he had both calmed down and revved up. He was calmer by putting some of his anticipations to rest. And his heart raced after seeing the size of the castle.

The door suddenly opened, and a tall lady in a navy-blue dress with a full skirt floated in. On the front of her hair was a tiny, sparkling diamond clip. She was followed by a man with a soft smile. Jack and his family all jumped to their feet.

Abernathy announced, "May I present the Earl of Moorland and Countess Virginia."

Everyone followed Abernathy's instructions and bowed or curtsied. When Jemima started to bend, she quickly changed her posture to a curtsey.

"Jackson Jones," the countess greeted as she glided toward them. "I am so glad you and your family were able to come. And, Rebecca Hampton, I am pleased you could join them." Then Lady Virginia bent down and cupped her hand under the dog's chin. "You too, Dutch. You are a beautiful, well-behaved four-legged friend."

Jackson bowed but kept an eye fixed on the additional royalty coming into the room. Jack smiled broadly at their son, who followed the Earl of Moorland.

The butler announced clearly, "May I present His Lordship's son, Lord Thomas, and the governess, Mrs. Wiggins."

The countess smiled at her daughter. "I am glad Gracie was able to show you around. Since we invited children for dinner, I thought our eldest two would like to join us for this meal. Lady Grace had lunch with the Princess Royal yesterday."

"Princess Royal?" Becky asked, then put her hand over her mouth. "I'm sorry, Countess Virginia. I shouldn't have asked."

"That is fine, Rebecca. And, you may call me, Ma'am," the countess said with a smile.

Jackson thought *Ma'am* seemed to be enjoying the company. When the countess started to smile a lot, he finally relaxed.

"A Princess Royal is the first-born daughter of the ruling King or Queen," the countess explained. "Lady Grace had a jolly good time with her cousin."

"The Princess Royal is your cousin?" Jemima asked Lady Grace.

"Indeed, she is," the countess answered with a chuckle. "Lord Thomas didn't go. It was a special time for the girls. Just like our younger two children are not old enough to eat at the table with us this evening. Lady Ann is a small baby. Ann and Timothy are in the nursery with Mrs. Kelley, the nanny. Mrs. Wiggins will check on them while we eat." The countess motioned to Abernathy to tell the servants to begin serving the meal.

"Yes, Ma'am," Becky said.

Jemima's mouth flew open in surprise as she bounced a little on her toes. "Crikey, Miss Grace, you know the Princess Royal."

"Mimee!" Her mum gasped as she slipped her hand under Jemima's arm to settle her down. "Hush."

Abernathy smiled, put his hand to the side of his mouth, and whispered, "Lady Grace finds the language a little stuffy, too."

"Crikey, I'm sorry," Jemima sighed.

Lady Grace said and grinned back at Jemima. "It is hard to remember all of this bowing and bending and names and words. Crikey."

Bridget cringed. "That word is becoming contagious."

"We have set the table in the family dining room," Lady Virginia said and gestured to the dining space in an adjoining alcove. The table, covered in a fine linen table cloth with matching napkins, sat in front of a large bay window. The glass facing the garden had multi panes from the floor to the high ceiling. "The formal dining room can seat many for dinner," she explained. "But I thought our family table would be large enough for us this evening. Do you not agree, Jackson Jones?"

"Yes, Ma'am," Jackson said, using the only words he could think of.

Countess Virginia silently rose and started toward the table. Abernathy raised his hand, indicating the guests should follow.

The butler reached for the dog leash. "I'll take Dutch to the kitchen. He can have dinner with the Fairmont dogs."

"Thank you. That will be the best meal my dog has ever had." Jackson handed Abernathy the end of the leather strap.

Jack stopped and looked around at the grandeur of the cream-colored Cozy Salon. Gold framed portraits hung on every wall of the sitting room. Jackson guessed they were pictures of the earl's family, not ancient ancestors. Over the fireplace was a portrait of Lady Virginia holding two of her puppies on her lap. Oil portraits of the children were arranged in an organized pattern around the room. One of the pictures was of baby Ann in her daddy's arms.

The ornate, gold ceiling had magnificently fixed crossbeams in the same valuable color as in the family dining room. Light and airy, white transparent curtains with blue accents flanked the bay window. A large oval carpet with blue and red flower blossoms covered the floor below a center chandelier of gold. Jackson had never seen anything this magnificent in all his life. While it was a family space, the earl and his family still dined in the splendor of a grand banquet.

"Jack," his mum motioned to him. "Move along."

As the butler pulled out his chair, the earl sat down. When the earl and his family sat at the table, Abernathy nodded. That was the cue for Jackson, and all those with him, to take their seats.

Jemima began to reach for a glass of water when her mother grabbed the sleeve on her bodice and pulled. Jemima folded her hands in her lap.

Young Lord Thomas also placed his hands in his lap and smiled at Jemima. "Crikey," he mouthed at her. His mother looked up but said nothing.

Jackson decided he was quite capable of eating politely at a table. But it would be safer to observe the countess and take his cues from her. If her Ladyship didn't touch anything, neither would he.

They had seen the Fairmont children's schoolroom right there in the castle. Rumors told the tail that their teacher taught them to use only the King's English, never common words or snappy slang. Jackson wondered if his family's speech would be a poor example for the children. His mouth flew open when the countess spoke again.

"Crikey," Virginia Fairmont teased. "I hope we can keep up with your new expressions."

Lady Grace giggled as she threw her hands to her mouth in surprise.

The earl smiled at his wife and reached for his son's hand on his right and Jackson's hand on the left, then bowed. "With those words spoken, let us offer grace."

Jackson smiled. He thought the earl's prayer over the food was as good as one of the Vicar's.

A bright serving girl in a long black dress, white apron, and small white hat brought in a fancy gold cart with a glass top. She took off bowls of steaming soup and placed one in front of the earl.

The countess smiled at the girl. "Kathleen will serve the food. She will also get anything you want or need that you do not see. She is an excellent worker and a fine young woman."

Jackson watched Kathleen gracefully lay out the first course of the meal. Jack noticed the earl kept his hands in his lap until the young woman served everyone. Jackson looked for his spoon so he wouldn't have to search for it when the signal came. He found it on the small plate under the soup bowl. The tomato soup was delicious. He had no idea what the cook put in it besides tomatoes, but it tasted nothing like anything he had eaten before.

Lady Grace moved her hand, knocking over her glass of juice, which spilled into her soup bowl and down onto her lap. "Oh no," she gasped.

"Do not worry, my dear," the countess said, patting Grace's hand. Lady Moorland pressed a button mounted to the table leg beside her. The button was attached to a wire connected to a series of bells in the kitchen and nursery. The governess returned and curtsied.

"Ma'am?"

The countess spoke softly. "Lady Grace has had an accident, Mrs. Wiggins. Please, take her to her room and help her change. She can join us again in a short while."

"Yes, Ma'am," the governess answered and helped the child push back the heavy dining room chair.

Lady Grace looked back at the table. "Will you walk with me, Jemima?"

Jemima nearly choked in surprise. "I would be happy to."

"Dear," the countess interrupted, "why doesn't Jemima walk to the kitchen with you so she can check on Dutch? Then she can come back to the table." Lady Moorland offered, "You'll be back in a few minutes."

"All right," Grace agreed.

Jackson was amazed when his little sister walked off with her new friend, Lady Grace, the eldest daughter of the Earl of Moreland.

Chapter Twenty-Three

In the Kitchen

Lady Grace reached for Jemima's hand as they walked from the dining room. Jemima felt close to Grace like she shared a great adventure with a new friend. Around a corner and down the hall, Jemima came to the kitchen and stood amazed. She had never seen a kitchen as large as the one in the castle. It was bigger than Mum's fireplace and hooks for pans in their cottage.

Dutch looked up only once when Jemima came in. His immediate task was eating, buried nose-deep in the best food ever laid out for people or pups.

"Hi Dutch," Jemima called out in a soft, melodic voice.

"Jemima," Grace said excitedly. "You sing when you talk."

"I do? Thank you, Miss."

"Miss?" the little lady curled up her nose. "Jemima, you're my friend. My name is Grace."

"Well, blimey," a familiar voice bellowed from the side door that led to the back courtyard. "If it isn't Jemima Jones."

Jemima shuddered. She knew who was behind her and, recognizing his voice, felt trapped. Which way could she run to hide?

"Digger," the cook said and nodded as she put a plate of food on the work table. It was only one of the many work surfaces in the large kitchen. "Are you nearly finished thatching His Lordship's small tool shed?"

Digger sat down on a stool and snugged up to the counter. "I'll be done tomorrow. It's late now," he said as he smiled when Lady Grace passed.

Jemima didn't like the way Digger looked at her new friend. "Digger, how did you come to work here?"

"Vicar Turner in Waddyshire said the earl's little cottage needed an odd-jobber for the day. I could use the money. I fixed some missing thatch for the earl about a year ago." Digger winked at Jemima as Mrs. Wiggins led Grace out of the room. "Bye-bye, little one," Digger drooled. Then he turned and wrapped his dirty hand around Jemima's wrist. "Stay and visit while I eat."

Jemima tried to free herself, but Digger Jinx would not let go. "Digger, I have to get back to the table. The countess is expecting me."

"Well, Bob's your uncle, and Fanny's your aunt," Digger mocked. "The great gentleman himself and his misses is waiting for the likes of you?"

Jemima pulled harder and looked at the cook for help. "Digger—"

"Is there a problem, Miss?" the round jolly lady asked in a not so cheery tone.

Jemima jerked her arm away as Digger weakened his grip. "No, Ma'am. No trouble. I have to get back to the table."

"Sorry," Digger apologized. "The young lady stopped me."

Jemima glared at Jinx, then hurried out of the kitchen. She was glad she was away from the dirty man. He often sat on the stone wall of the cemetery. He would watch as Jemima and her school friends walked home. Digger frightened her in Waddyshire, and he scared her in Lochlan.

Chapter Twenty-Four

Dining with the Earl

Jackson heard every creak in the castle. When Jemima inched back into the dining room, Jack felt relieved. All were where they belonged except Grace. As Jemima sat down, the countess was talking.

Lady Virginia paused and smiled when she saw that Jemima was back. The countess continued. "I'm glad my keeper of the horses was able to find you, Jackson." She sat back so a servant could pat the table cloth dry following Lady Grace's accident.

The earl prepared to eat a bite of soup. "Our senior horseman is very good."

Jemima picked up her spoon. "What is a senior horseman and keeper of the horses?"

The earl noticed that Jackson took in all the information about racing. The earl's soft eyes revealed his pleasure in Jack's joy in learning all he could. "You and your sister ask good questions," he laughed. "Our keeper of the livery is in charge of our entire stable, from the carriage horses, the riding mounts, the hunting steeds, and my racehorses," the earl answered. "That's why I invited all of you. Jackson, you were the winner of our annual Derby. The race was founded in 1780 by the 12th Earl of Derby." The earl paused and sipped at his soup without making a single slurping sound.

Oliver's eyes twinkled. "You love the horses too, I think, Sir."

"Oh yes," the earl said with a loving smile. "My thoroughbreds have often won the race at Craggy Crook Downs." Suddenly his face contorted. "Mrs. Wiggins? What's wrong?"

A castle servant would never have darted back into the room as the governess had. She would have entered so quietly no one would have known she was there. "Ma'am, Sir," Wiggins gasped. "Is Lady Grace in here?"

"In here?" The earl questioned sharply.

Mrs. Wiggins wrung her hands, and her voice trembled in worry. "I was taking Lady Grace to her room to change her dress. After leaving the kitchen, we stopped at the Conservatory for just a minute. We watched the songbirds sing as they flew from branch to branch." She swallowed hard. "I turned around, and she was gone. I can't find her."

Jackson wondered why they seemed concerned. In Waddyshire, he and Jemima were everywhere: the village, into the woods, and up the mountainside. Yes, the castle was much larger than his family's home. But that was all the more reason why Grace was safe. She could run around through the castle halls without leaving her home.

"Jackson," Jemima kicked Jack's leg under the table. "Digger Jinx was in the kitchen."

"Digger?" Jack whispered gruffly. "Digger Jinx?" he nearly shouted as he turned to the earl. *Now I'm worried.* "Sir, Jemima said there is a man in the kitchen. All the children in Waddyshire are afraid of him."

The earl ordered Abernathy, "Send a guard to the kitchen and find the man, Digger Jinx."

The earl jumped up from his chair and put his arm around his wife. "I authorized the hiring of the odd-jobber, Jinx, to fix the thatch. He was recommended highly by someone at the church."

"He is a good worker," Oliver offered. "He repaired the thatch on our roof."

Jack figured his pa vouched for Digger more to comfort the countess than to say anything positive about Jinx.

When the guard came back to report to the earl about Digger, the whole room let out a fearful sigh. "The man is gone. He isn't anywhere."

Lady Virginia quickly turned to the guard. "Could he have taken Grace with him? Send for the seer. We must find him immediately."

"Yes, ma'am." The guard bowed. "The seer was at the fair. I know his store."

"Take a horse and bring him here." The countess waved her hand, dismissing the guard. To the family, she added. "Lady Grace likes to play in the castle. Wandering through the rooms, she sometimes gets lost. I'm sure she is fine, maybe she's lost down a long hall. We'll find her. And our seer will help locate her."

"Your seer?" Bridget asked.

"Yes." The earl drummed his fingertips together. Then he admitted, "The church is not pleased with his mystical powers, but my page introduced him. I find him interesting." He paused and picked up his spoon. "Please, finish your soup before it gets any colder."

Jackson watched as everyone followed the countess's movements and finished their first course. When the servants brought in roasted chicken and rice, Jackson could not believe the size of each serving. The chicken was golden and smelled of rich browned crust. Not wanting to stare at the food, he snuck a peek at each plate. Sauteed mushrooms and asparagus in breadcrumbs were both served. As soon as Lady Virginia picked up her fork, Jack had his in his hand. Still, with every bite, he thought of Lady Grace and the fact that Digger Jinx was in the castle. Was the little girl safe? Would the Vicar have recommended Digger if children were in danger around him?

Chapter Twenty-Five

Lady Grace is Missing

Just as Jackson finished his scrumptious dessert of bread-and-butter Pudding, Mrs. Wiggins quietly stepped into the room. At first, Jack paid little attention as the aroma of nutmeg still clung to the crumbs on his plate. He snapped to attention when he saw Mrs. Wiggins' expression become serious.

"Oh, good, Wiggins," the countess whispered as she sat back in relief. "Where did you find her?"

"No, Ma'am." Mrs. Wiggins' voice cracked in fear and anxiety. "We haven't found Lady Grace yet." The children's governess whispered even lower, wringing her hands, "And, the guards just told me they have detected another intruder."

Jackson certainly heard that pronouncement. The previous year, an intruder had crept into the castle like a thief in the night. All of the newspapers carried the story. Jack suspected the evil one was there to attempt an assassination. Whoever he was, the trespasser didn't have a copper tuppence for the butler at the front door. What the intruder did have, was a plan for something. Perhaps he wanted to kill or capture the earl and even his family. Maybe his plan included destroying Jackson Jones and those who sat in the castle laughing and enjoying a meal around the table.

"Another one? How is that possible?" the earl asked in horror. "Perhaps he's just after the diamond," he said as he grasped another thought.

The countess shook her head in disbelief. "Everyone knows the Diamond of the East would not be in our castle. We had it here for one day as part of a fundraising exhibition. The diamond is part of the Crown Jewels, so it is inside the vault in Lochlan. That diamond belongs to the queen, a gift from the king."

Oliver folded his napkin and placed it on the table. "Perhaps we should go, Your Lordship. You are taking care of serious matters right now."

Lady Virginia beckoned her guard to come closer. "How is the search going for our daughter and the trespasser? Would it be safe for Jackson and his family to leave?"

"My dear," the earl began with a deep sigh, "the trespasser, as you call him, is not here to sit in my smoking room and smoke one of my cigars. Nor do I think he is after the diamond." He said no more but looked intently at his wife.

"No, Ma'am," the guard said as he straightened stiffly. "I don't think your guests should leave until we find the intruder and Lady Grace."

"Well, good then," the earl said firmly. "Let us retire to the chairs in the Cozy Salon. We can play dominoes while we wait for the all-clear signal. The children can play on the floor and the adults at the game table."

"Ma'am, are you sure?" Bridget asked.

The countess smiled. "I am always sure, Mrs. Jones." And with that, she got up and walked over to a wingback chair covered in a light blue fabric with gold piping and trim.

Jackson wanted to ask the same question. He was not a boy to sit around and wait while others cared for him. "If Lady Grace wandered off and got lost, Becky and I could help look for her. Becky is great with children."

"That is very nice of you, Jackson." Countess Virginia sat at the game table near the white marble fireplace. "But there are one-hundred seventy-five rooms in the castle."

Quickly, Jack's expression changed to alarm as his eyebrows rose. "Listen!"

Bridget jumped when her son suddenly burst out. "Jack," she stammered.

"No, Mrs. Jones," the countess ordered, trembling with fear. "What is it, Jackson? What do you hear?"

"Doesn't anyone hear someone crying?" Jackson searched the faces of all those at the table. Everyone had blank expressions except Becky. She seemed to be as sensitive as Jack. "The crying, Your Ladyship," Jackson said, his head down and his right ear listening toward the hall.

Heads shook. "No."

"It has to be Grace. Who else would be crying?" The countess began to stand up when suddenly an icy wind started to blow through the castle halls. "We have sealed many of the rooms right now."

"Yes, Ma'am," Becky chimed in. "I can hear her, too. Who else would call out, 'Help Mummy? I'm cold,' and then cry?"

Her Ladyship explained, "The upper rooms of the castle started freezing the other day. I ordered all of them sealed."

"Virginia," the earl interrupted as he looked at the guard. "The seer has arrived."

"Show him in," the countess ordered the guard. "The seer will know when Mr. Barker came to see me and told me about the wind in Waddyshire. He—" She took out a handkerchief and blotted her eyes. "He told me of a great deer in your area. The deer told one of my huntsmen—"

"A deer told you, Ma'am?" Bridget stammered.

"Please, Mum," Jackson dismissed with the palms of his hands on the table. "I know the deer. It was Mighty Red, wasn't it?"

The earl's mouth gaped. "Yes, that's what Mr. Barker called him." He threw his hand to his chest and breathed deeply. Blotting his eyes again, he nearly choked as he cleared his throat. "Jackson, I need you. I don't know what you can do, but Mr. Barker said you are the one. Are you the one Jackson Jones?"

Chapter Twenty-Six

The One

"The one what?" Bridget and Oliver asked sternly, both demanding an answer from the earl.

"Wait!" Oliver shushed in a raspy voice. "I apologize, Your Lordship. But he is our son. We must know why you really invited us here."

"Jackie," Becky jumped up and stomped her foot. "Tell them the *one what*," she demanded.

"Mum…Pa, I am not lying." Jackson shook his head slowly, almost in disbelief, even though the deer spoke to him, too. "I…do not know what or who *the one* is."

"I believe him," the earl announced. "The deer is…a monarch red deer. The King is our monarch and my cousin, and you, you are *the one*. You are the one to defeat the Shaman-fey, and you are the one to bring our sweet Gracie back to us."

"Your Lordship, you brought us here to celebrate more than Jackson's win at the Derby. What do you want from our son?" Oliver was respectful, but he would get the answers.

"As I said," the earl spoke softly, as he began wringing his hands, "the upper rooms here in the castle began to freeze. At first, we didn't know what was happening."

"Then, Gracie became the target," the earl admitted. "One morning, ice sealed her door all the way around. I called in our blacksmith. He was able to bring a bucket of hot coals from the forge, melt the ice, and free our precious little girl."

"That was wise," Oliver nodded.

"This morning," the countess's eyes kept darting toward the hall, "I went to the room where we had moved Grace. I wanted to awaken her. The wind swirled like an icy blast through the hall just outside her room. I burst through her door, hurried to the leaded windows, and released the latch to let the morning heat flood her room. We have never had any of the rooms get that cold. There is another reason for the chill. Jackson, the Shaman-fey is in Lochlan. Our page told us."

Bridget squared her shoulder and leaned in toward the countess. "What does that have to do with Jackson?"

The earl looked intently at Jack. "Mr. Barker said the deer told him it was Jackson Jones who stopped the Nordic blast above Waddyshire." The earl spoke firmly. "He said the deer told him—"

"Pardon me, Sir," Jack apologized as he jumped to his feet.

The countess's eyes grew large as she looked up at the boy who now towered over her. Abernathy lunged in

Jack's direction, but Her Ladyship raised her hand and stopped him. "No…Abernathy. Let him speak." She turned to Jackson. "Please, young man, sit down."

"Yes, Ma'am," he blushed. "Mr. Barker probably told you that I am the one who played the night music that finally calmed the Shaman-fey."

"And, you take the horn everywhere with you," the countess added, pointing to the pouch. "I suppose that is the golden horn."

"Gold!" Jemima blurted.

"Yes, Mimee," Jack assured her. "My horn is gold."

"Please, play it," the countess begged. "The Shaman-fey is in the castle. I know it."

"But, Ma'am," Jackson pulled at the chord on the pouch and gripped it more closely. "If I go up and down the halls playing sweet music, it will soothe many, but the Shaman's evil will grow stronger. The Shaman will weaken if I play sad, mournful melodies, but others who hear it will become sick, maybe deathly ill."

"May I go with him, Father?" Lord Thomas pleaded.

"Absolutely not. You heard what Jackson said. It's not safe," the earl said firmly.

"You're saving your son but not mine?" Oliver snapped.

"No, Sir." The earl's shoulders slumped, and tears gathered in his eyes. "I am so sorry I was not clear. I didn't mean to value our son over yours."

The countess put her hand to her mouth. Her voice trembled. "Please, no. It isn't safe for Tommy, and it isn't safe for your son, Jackson. But, what can we do?"

"Pa," Jackson pleaded, "I must help find Lady Grace. And I have to stop the Shaman-fey again. I must save the castle, the earl, his family, and Arie itself. If I am the one who can do it, I must."

"I know you're right, Jack," Oliver admitted with his face etched in worry lines. "But you're young, and young men aren't always aware of the danger."

"I have faced the Shaman before, Pa." Jackson's eyes were downcast. "I will be careful."

Oliver sighed deeply. "The Kingdom has to be safe."

"I will look for her, too," Mrs. Wiggins announced with determination as she turned and left the room.

Jackson's eyebrows raised in alarm. "I hear Lady Grace. Her voice sounds more frightened than before." He looked at his parents and insisted, "I have to help her."

Chapter Twenty-Seven
On the Hunt

Abernathy entered again with a tall thin man close behind. The skinny bloke looked familiar to Jackson.

"Madam, the seer is here." Abernathy stepped aside as Fastidious Fog entered. Fog bowed so low he nearly landed on the floor.

"Mr. Fog," the countess exhaled deeply, "you came. Thank you."

"Fastidious Fog!" Jackson gasped. "We met you at the fair, and you were there at Froggy Bottom's."

"Yes, young Jackson Jones. I remember." As Fog talked, his long greying goatee bobbed up and down.

"Does that tickle?" Jemima asked.

"Mimee!" Bridget snapped at the child in a stern voice. "It's not polite to ask personal questions."

"I understand, Missus." Mr. Fog said with a weak smile. "I had a daughter, too."

Jackson was thinking like Jemima. He wanted to ask Fog what his daughter's name was and what he meant when he said, "I had a daughter." But his mum had already said it wasn't polite to ask personal questions.

"Mr. Fog," the countess began, "our daughter Grace spilled her juice. As Mrs. Wiggins took her back to the nursery, Grace must have walked off. We cannot find her."

Suddenly, Jackson heard scuffling coming from deep in the castle. The noise came from somewhere down the long marble hall and echoed around the building. Looking around at the others in the Cozy Salon, fear had suddenly gripped their faces.

Lord Moorland dashed to his wife and stood between her and whoever lurked in the massive castle. At the same time, several guards charged in and surrounded the earl while some guarded the door, their rifles held ready.

From a distance, there was the thump of running feet and voices yelling, "Halt! Stop, or I'll fire!"

"Get outa my way!" returned a deep, gravelly voice.

Those in the drawing-room held their breath. Motionless, except for arms thrown around each other as they huddled together in stiffened silence, Becky clung to Jack's arm.

The sounds of fighting and people falling on the marble floor came closer to the room. Some smacked onto the hard alabaster, and others thudded heavily on the carpet as they rolled and tumbled.

Running feet tramped faster and faster. "Your Lordship," the head guard interrupted as he rushed into the drawing-room. "The intruder has been captured."

The countess collapsed back in her chair in relief. "Did you find out how he got in?"

"We believe so, Ma'am." Standing tall and rigid, the guard spoke sharply. "But the culprit is not saying. He was in the halls on the south side of the castle. The master gardener planted shrubs close to the building on that side, with many large clumps of trees. The man's clothes were black, from his cap to his shoes."

"Thank you," the earl breathed deeply.

The danger has passed, Jackson thought as he looked down at Becky. He nodded. She nodded back in agreement.

Jackson darted out of the room with his horn over his shoulder. Before anyone could stop her, Becky was on his heels.

"Becky!" Bridget gasped. "No!"

Oliver rose to his feet, grabbed Bridget by the shoulders, and gently kissed the top of her head. "They have to go. If the Shaman-fey harms Lady Grace, his rage will not stop there. He'll come on through and wipe out the earl and all of us."

Fastidious Fog began to pace. "I am the seer," Fog reported with determination. "I must follow Jackson. I can help find Lady Grace."

"Hurry, please," the countess said quickly. "Catch up to them. You can find my daughter."

"You protect her well, my Lady," Fog said with a small smile. "Anyone would protect their daughter," Fastidious Fog said with an awkward sound of sympathy in his voice.

"That's right, Mr. Fog," Oliver said. "You had a daughter too. What was her name?"

Fog's eyes avoided his gaze. A hint of caring crossed his face like he remembered loving his daughter deeply. When he spoke, his voice cracked in two, half in pain, half in love. "I called her, Little-Lovie."

Chapter Twenty-Eight

Another Way to the Top

In the hall, Fastidious Fog slipped off to the left. Fog knew the bedrooms would be on the second floor. He figured there had to be more than one way to get upstairs. Most people visiting the home used the magnificent stairs famous to the castle, the Broadmoor staircase.

The back staircase was magnificent, although the width of the treads was not nearly as wide as the main staircase, and the curve was less spectacular than the one in the center of the castle. Fog dashed up the steps, two at a time, ignoring the magnificent stained-glass window as he turned at the landing. The Earl of Mooreland's Coat of Arms, held in the glass by lead channels, proudly loomed above a figure of a man dressed in complete royal regalia. But Fog saw nothing. The frigid air grew icier the higher he climbed.

As he moved up to the bedroom floor, the frost that clung to each doorknob and jamb was a guidepost that directed him to the coldest room.

Why had the Shaman picked the nursery to attack? Of all the rooms in the castle, the children's room was the least threatening to an anger-filled man. The main job of children is to grow, learn, laugh, and love.

As he walked down the hall, Fog's face froze in determination. No one would stop him. He had reasons to find the child, and no one else needed to know why. He was on a quest. He would be the one to find Lady Grace.

Chapter Twenty-Nine
The Blueprints

Oliver took Bridget's hand in his. "My dear, I have seen Jack play that horn. There are ways to protect yourself from the effects of the sorrowful music."

"There are?" Abernathy's expression changed from fear to shock.

"Abernathy?" The earl asked through gritted teeth. "What do you know about all of this?"

"Me?" The butler swallowed hard. "Nothing, Sir." He gulped again.

"Yes, you do. Tell me." The earl demanded gruffly. "You directed the planting of the trees. The very ones that allowed the intruder a way to get it. Now, your expression reveals your involvement."

"Sir…I've known a man since I was a boy. He told me I had to help him get inside the castle…or—"

The earl leaned his knuckles on the table. "Or, or what?"

"Or…he'd tell everyone. I was the one who broke the ice, sending the Farrier's son, Jonathon, to the bottom of the lake," Abernathy blurted. "But I didn't mean for him to get hurt. He was stuck out there on the hard surface of the lake, and I crawled out, hoping to save him."

"And the man has blackmailed you," the earl concluded.

The countess shook her head in disbelief. "We'll deal with that later," Her Ladyship soothed. "For now…I believe you, Abernathy." She folded her hands in her lap.

"I gave him the blueprints to the castle." Abernathy wiped his brow and quickly added, "but that is all I gave him."

"The guards are on full alert," Lady Moorland said with her jaw set, and her back stiffened. "He didn't get very far. For now, what else must we know?"

"The man I gave the blueprints to," Abernathy stuttered, "is my cousin, Edward. He has an antique shop in Lochlan and thought it would be nice to frame the blueprints and hang them in the shop as decoration."

"The blueprints to our home?" the earl bellowed.

"Now, I realize how stupid I was." Abernathy's eyes filled with tears. Then his expression softened a little. "The Shaman-Cherish is in the castle, too. I don't know where she is, and I don't know why she's here." Abernathy began wringing his hands. "But she is good."

I know," the countess agreed, smiling weakly. "She's the Shaman of Love. She can only bring peace. When I was a child, I would see her gliding through the garden like she was floating. Everything she touched burst into bloom."

"Why is she here?" Bridget asked, her face contorted in fear for the safety of all of the children.

Abernathy's gaze dropped to the floor. Sobbing deeply, he stammered, "Cherish has always been a friend of Mr. Fog. At least they were friends when Mr. Fog's daughter was still alive. Maybe Fastidious asked her to come and calm the Shaman-fey."

"Can Cherish stop the Shaman-fey?" Young Lord Thomas asked, dropping his head to his folded hands on the table.

Abernathy shook his head in surrender. "Forgive me. I am so sorry. There's nothing any of us can do."

"There are two things that can be done," Oliver soothed. "When Jackson plays any happy, uplifting tunes, inhale the magic of the strength that floats on the notes. They will prepare you for any mournful themes he may have to play. If, and when, sad music comes from his horn, have ready something to cover your ears. A little of the music will get through but not enough to do harm. The other thing is what my son will do." Oliver's expression changed to a soft, assuring smile. Oliver said. "You will see. You don't know my son, Jack, and the magic of his golden horn."

Chapter Thirty

Where?

Jackson and Becky turned the wrong way when they ran out of the Cozy Salon. They darted into the kitchen, which turned out to be a good move. When they walked in, Kathleen, the serving girl, was helping the cook over at the wood-burning cast-iron stove. Dutch was still in the room.

Dutch pranced around the earl's dogs when he saw Jackson. The collie's toenails clicked on the red brick floor and caused the girl to turn.

Kathleen jumped in surprise. "Oh my, Mr. Jones. You didn't have to come into the kitchen to get something. I would have been happy to bring it to you."

"No, Kathleen," Becky said as her eyes scanned the entire room. "We're looking for Lady Grace."

"The little Lady?" Kathleen looked at the round-in-the-middle cook. "Mrs. Wiggins took Lady Grace to her room to change her clothes. Is something wrong?"

Jackson started to move on through the kitchen. "Come, Dutch." He knew the dog might sniff out what he couldn't. He shouted to Kathleen over his shoulder. "Lady Grace is missing."

Chapter Thirty-One

Searching

The Broadmoor Staircase

Everyone in southern Arie knew the Broadmoor Staircase was the most beautiful in the shire. Jackson and Becky hurried quietly down the Marble Hall toward the stairs. All along their way, a thick red-carpet runner of the finest wool allowed no squeaking or footfalls on the polished marble floor. A few elegant gold tables with sparkling white marble tops stood along both sides of the hall. Jack and Rebecca looked everywhere. But Gracie was not hiding *under*, *behind*, or *in* anything.

Jackson tapped Becky's shoulder and whispered, "Be careful. Digger Jinx is around here, too."

Becky's face grew tight with fear. "He could have grabbed Lady Grace already."

Jack stopped and grew ridged. "We might have to find her first and then rescue her."

"How?" Becky mouthed as lines of panic formed beside her eyes.

Jackson shrugged and moved on. "We'll figure it out."

Fit for a massive home, the curved Broadmoor staircase rose to the floor above. Jackson and Rebecca had walked past the stairs when Abernathy first directed them to the Cozy Salon.

Jack and Becky started up the steps. They got a full view of the paintings hanging on the wood-paneled walls, the marble columns, and the gilded ceiling with all its decorative wood from the landing above. Becky looked down, bent, and picked up something from a stair tread. Then she brought the clump up to her face to study it more closely. She shrugged and handed it to Jackson.

Dirt on the carpet? Jackson couldn't believe his eyes. First, the cleaning staff would never have left something on the floor. Second, Jack had focused on something so small while Lady Grace remained lost. Instantly, he recognized the piece of nothing he held. His breath caught in his throat. *Thatch*!

The Reception Room

As they eased across the upper landing, Jackson looked down at all the treads they had climbed and listened to the hallway around them. Hansel and Gretel had not run up those steps. There was no evidence of evil anywhere, no sound of crying, and no dropped bread crumbs. Still, the little Lady had to be in the castle somewhere.

The two searchers slipped into the Reception Room. Stepping slowly and lightly, they tiptoed across the carpet beneath enormous crystal chandeliers.

The staff had not prepared the room for a special event, so chairs casually lined the walls. Jackson motioned to Becky. "I know some of the chairs have open arms, and all are open underneath, but check for Grace anyway. We'll both feel better."

Even though it was easy to see there was nothing under the chairs and sofas, Becky and Jackson stooped over and searched under everything.

"Should we?" Jackson asked as he stood in front of one of the chests against the wall.

"Are you going to open the earl's closed cabinets?" Becky's voice was soft, but her eyes screamed at Jackie.

"Becky, we have to," Jack insisted. But when he opened the double-facing doors, there was no little lady. There were only several candlesticks and other items to prepare the room for guests. "She's not here," he said.

When Jackson turned, he saw Becky looking through another cabinet. She showed him her empty hands.

Jack drummed his fingers on the top of the cabinet as he looked around the room. "I'll check the fireplace." It was so empty in the middle he couldn't see how anyone could hide in there, but he would check.

"Jackson Jones," Becky firmly put her hands on her hips, "if Lady Grace is in the fireplace, she has turned into smoke and is floating up the chimney."

"I know, I know," Jack admitted. "But, if she's in danger, we need to find her fast."

When Becky turned, her mouth dropped open. "Jackie, look," Becky said as she held her breath while she pointed.

"It's the Ball Room." As he peered through a wide opening into the next room, Jackson could see two impressive Windsor chairs. His heart began to beat harder.

The Ball Room

Jackson stood silently at the door to the Ball Room. He knew it was special, but it was more than that. It felt sacred. Then he realized his respect for his country and its leaders caused those feelings. He wiggled his finger to coax Rebecca to follow him into the room.

They entered through tall white doors with gold trim that led off the Reception Room. Jackson gulped and whispered, "Thank goodness it's open. I don't like possible surprises behind closed doors."

Becky grabbed her stomach as they crept along the room's perimeter like mice on a hunt. They searched both sides of the room and under the chairs.

"I know," Jackson agreed as his insides tightened and churned. Waves of guilt overtook him. He was invading the earl's rooms where high government officials met.

The two stepped with weary toes up the three steps that led to the musicians' small stage. Jackson could not think of another way to look for Gracie. He and Becky had to ransack Arie's fanciest spaces. With muscles developed at the anvil in his father's forge, Jack lifted the chairs and pulled back the curtain hanging from the ceiling to the floor behind it.

Rebecca flipped the heavy drapery back and forth, looking for anyone who could hide in its folds. "Where is she?" Becky whispered.

In front of the tall wall of windows, backless gold cushioned benches waited for a guest to rest. Six additional, smaller chairs lined the side walls under gilded ceilings. Jackson did not sit down.

Jack scanned around the room. "There's nothing here." His whisper was so low and desperate he could barely hear his own words while his thoughts raced on.

The Ball Room was beautiful, but no one was there except the visions that Jack could imagine. In his mind, a string orchestra played for those who danced on the shiny hardwood floor. Jackson wondered if his horn would let him play with the other musicians or would the golden horn continue to play its own melodies.

The Library

Jackson led the way down another hall. Elegant paintings hung on both sides. Jackson didn't know the names of the painters, but he had seen pictures of the masterpieces in a book at the Waddyshire School library. While he usually preferred pictures of dogs, Jack knew it was a privilege to come close to the treasured works of art. He wondered why the Shaman hadn't demanded money for the return of Lady Grace. The earl certainly had enough money that a ransom wouldn't hurt his bank account.

None of the doors along the side walls leading to other rooms were open except the tall one at the end of the hall. Jackson and Becky inched toward the room and stood for a moment before going in. With so many shelves full of books of all sizes, several desks, and comfortable chairs by the windows, it was easy to see they found the library.

"Look at all the books," Becky gasped, holding her breath. "They have a library, here, in their own home."

Jackson whispered and pointed to an elaborate desk. "The earl probably sits at that desk and researches ideas for his inventions."

"The countess may have started writing a new book. Besides her painting, I heard she is an author. But she uses another name." Rebecca told him.

Jack shook his head in disbelief. "These two are very talented."

"Look along the floor," Becky said and pointed with a grin. "Picture books have been pulled out and stacked in neat piles."

"The children have been reading in here," Jackson agreed. The slight pungent odor of dog treats came from some half-eaten pieces crunched underfoot along the side.

"It looks like the family's Dachshund, Jip, was here too." Becky bent and started to clean up the crumbs.

"The dog's name is Jip?" Jackson asked as he stopped to think about the name. "Jip means to cheat someone."

"For a dog," Becky corrected him, "Jip is a Dutch name. It means, "She who sings.""

"Sings?" Jackson blurted-out. "Dogs can't sing."

Becky smiled a little and looked under the desk again. "Jackie, maybe Jip can."

"I know," Jackson agreed.

Becky's breath escaped in fear. "Look," she shuddered as she pointed to the floor near the edge of the desk. Becky got down as close to the carpet as possible. Looking back at Jackson, she gasped, "It's more thatch." She picked it up and rubbed it between her fingers. "The room is empty now. Where is Grace?"

Suddenly, Jack heard something from inside the building. "Listen."

"What is it?" Becky tipped her head to hear whatever Jackson detected. "I can't hear anything."

"I don't know yet," Jack said as he quickly took in as much as possible.

Becky looked at the book titles on the desk, one by one. "There are many people in the castle. Someone here has recently changed their reading interest to the Druids."

"Druids?" Jackson wondered why that ancient topic had piqued someone's interest. His words faded away until he barely spoke. Then the faint sound of crying filtered again through the halls.

Many Bedrooms

Next, they entered a suite of rooms that had to be those of the earl and countess. Within the space, two bedrooms flowed into a common-sitting room. Jackson felt guilty snooping around.

"Hum," Jackson thought it odd. "Mum and Pa have just one room." But there was no time for musing. They had a child to find.

Dutch sniffed around until his nose pushed open a short door to Jip's bedroom. A low bed with a feather comforter and matching pillow lay in the corner beside a crystal water bowl.

Jackson shook his head in amazement. "Don't even dream about it, Dutch."

Becky's eyes widened. "I could sleep in Jip's bedroom."

Nothing appeared under the beds, in the wardrobe, armoire, or behind the drapes. Jackson squared his shoulders. "There are many guest rooms to search. We'd better hurry on."

"Jackie?" Becky asked as she looked around. "Where do the children sleep?"

Jack's eyes brightened. "Mrs. Wiggins said she would take Grace to the nursery."

Chapter Thirty-Two

The Nursery

Back in the hall, Becky nudged Jackson's arm. "Look." She pointed toward an eerie, icy glow from a room on the left, at the end of the hall.

Jackson remained silent, put his finger to his lips, and motioned to Becky. They would have to walk into the ghastly frost. They edged down the hall to a room that drew him like a magnet to iron. Icicles formed on the door and hung above the jamb like stalactites in a deep cave.

Becky slipped up beside Jack. Together, they stopped just outside the door, took a deep breath, and turned the knob.

The L-shaped room had two large sections. Where they entered was a play area. It had toys, picture books, a hobby horse, and shelves of games. A fluffy white carpet was on the center of the floor.

"Must be the nursery," Jackson determined when he looked around and saw a dollhouse. A horse and carriage, drawn up to the front door of the miniature, Victorian home with its high-pitched roof, waited to take a doll family wherever they wanted to go.

Dutch crawled into the room, scooting on the floor. With a low growl, his eyes stayed fixed on the back of the room.

Jack whispered, "Dutch, stay."

Rebecca was paying no attention to Dutch. She was inspecting every inch of the little Victorian structure. She was too old to play with the house and its tiny furniture, but she could still be amazed by a building so typical of Lochlan homes. "I've never seen anything like it."

The tiny architecture looked nothing like the thatched-roof cottages of Waddyshire. Bric-a-brac accents snugged up under the tall peak of the Victorian dormer window.

"The toy store on Merriweather Lane has nothing like this," Jack whispered. "I think the white frame house was made just for the earl's children. Maybe the earl made it himself."

Jack looked down at Dutch. The dog's ears were pinned back to his head. "What is wrong, boy?"

Becky stopped and gasped when she moved into the longer length of the sectioned-off room. Her eyes, drawn tight in fear, darted from child to child.

The scene was terrifying. Four-and-a-half-year-old Timothy had climbed into the crib and was holding baby Ann tightly in his arms. The infant was sleeping and had no awareness of the danger that stalked the nursery. Perhaps it was Timothy who needed the closeness of the cuddly baby to soothe his fears. He sat cross-legged in the corner of the crib, whimpering.

Jackson's breath stopped in his throat, like a lump of his mum's bread that was too big to swallow. He could feel his heart pounding against his ribs. Lady Grace sat in a small chair beside the crib near the nursery room window. There was terror in her eyes.

The little girl's hands were bound in Fastidious Fog's strong grip. Lady Grace could not pull her fingers away. Fog seethed with anger. Mrs. Wiggins lay unconscious on the floor in the corner of the room. Under one of Fog's feet was the body of Digger Jinx. The sharp thatch knife was still in Digger's hand, but he couldn't use it in his state. Fog's foot was on Digger's neck, and ice formed in Jinx's hair. Grace's entire body shivered from being so near Digger's freezing body.

Fog festered with anger. "Jinx broke into the castle. He found the little one in the hall." Fog pressed his foot harder. "Then, he dragged her in here."

"Mr. Fog?" Jackson questioned. He was confused and frightened by the look in Fog's eyes. "You followed them into the nursery and saved Lady Grace from Digger?"

"Ah, there he is," Fog spit out, grinding the heel of his shoe into Digger when he moved a little. "The boy with the golden horn, who plays lilting tunes for some and terrible dirges of fear and death for others."

"You know of my horn?" Jackson asked. "How?" His mind raced to catch up with what his eyes saw.

Fastidious Fog sneered. "Everyone knows about the music, Jackson."

Jackson's focus stayed on the children. He had trouble clearing his mind, rearranging the tangled cluster of thought threads that twisted and turned into knotted conclusions. "Are you protecting Lady Grace from Digger Jinx? Did you stop him from taking her away?"

Fog's eyes penetrated clear through Jackson's armor of positive strength. "What do you think, young rescuer of all the people?"

Did Digger Jinx stop Fog from rescuing Grace, or did Fog stop Jinx from capturing Grace? Jackson didn't know what to think. He didn't even know which one was the villain.

Chapter Thirty-Three
The Sweet Music

Fastidious Fog hissed through gritted teeth. When Digger Jinx stirred under his foot, Fog stomped his shoe again. Pulling on Grace's arm, Fog growled, "She belongs with me. But Fiona doesn't want to come home."

.   "Fiona?" Jackson gulped as he realized, *Fastidious Fog is the Shaman-fey!* Jack screamed in silence. He fumbled for the drawstring on the leather pouch.

"Please…" Becky spoke with a calming, melodic lilt to her voice. "Please, let go of Lady Grace. I'd be happy to take her back to her parents for you. Thank you, Mr. Fog, for finding her."

Jack couldn't believe it. Didn't Rebecca hear what Fog said? The man got Grace mixed up with his own daughter, Fiona.

Rebecca reached out to take the child, but the Shaman's knuckles only whitened more. Lady Grace winced and tried to pull her arm out of the Fog's grasp.

"No!" The Shaman-fey bellowed as snow-like ice pebbles blasted sleet from his mouth.

Rebecca jumped back with a look of terror on her face. Her eyes darted from Fog to Jackie.

Jackson did not flinch as he fixed his eyes like flint on the monster. Jack reached into his pouch for the horn. His body nearly folded in on itself, trying not to move one unnecessary muscle.

Rebecca shot a glance at Jack and nodded. She moved stiffly, trying to hide her actions, and pulled a cotton handkerchief from her pocket. She tore off two corners and hid them in her fists. As Jackson brought the horn to his lips and puckered, Becky quickly put the pieces of cloth in her ears.

Jackson first played a few happy, uplifting music bars to strengthen those within hearing before the angry notes began. Then, Jack knew he had to think of what made him sad. He thought of the day the neighbor's horse trampled Dutch, nearly killing him. The whole experience filled Jackson's mind with fear and grief. He knew the notes would weaken the Shaman. But would it harm Lady Grace? What about the other two children and everyone else within hearing. Jackson blew his thoughts into the horn. After only three musical bars, little Grace began to wretch, but Rebecca couldn't reach her.

Suddenly, a dim light filled the room and grew in brilliance. A figure in a shimmering white gown floated through the shining. The graceful beauty's hands swayed to the rhythm of the music. Jeweled rings sparkled on the spirit's fingers, and bells twinkled on her toes as she moved in time with the melodies. As Jackson played the sad and grief-filled notes, music lilted from the figure in the center of the radiance. The progression was soft and loving:

Becky heard the music through the cotton in her ears. The melody filtered through Jack's notes, but he continued to play his anguish-filled dirge.

"Fastidious," the voice sang out in a quiet tone.

"No!" Fog screamed back. "Go away!"

"Dear Fastidious," the beautiful woman of the light whispered. "Let Grace go."

Fog tightened his grip on Grace until she cried out in pain. "Cherish, leave!" he demanded.

Jackson stopped blowing into the horn long enough to ask, "Cherish?"

"Cherish?" Rebecca repeated. "The Shaman of Love?"

Cherish smiled and spoke to Fastidious. "You remember Fiona. I heard you call her Little Lovie." Cherish's voice filled with joy as she sang out, "Lovie was that and more." She stopped for a second and turned to Jackson. "Play the beautiful notes. The sweet and loving ones."

Jackson stopped for a second. What should he do? The sweet notes would calm everyone in the castle. But what about Fog? In the past, the lovely notes only filled Fog with more anger and gave him the power to send out more ice and frigid cold. Still, there was something warm and trusting in Cherish's eyes. Jackson put the golden horn to his mouth again and thought of the earl's children and their happy laughter in the castle's halls. He thought of how Fiona may have looked. Mr. Fog had called her Little Lovie.

Jackson knew nothing about Fiona or how old she was. But he knew her name. To Becky, he whispered, "Think of anything pretty, loving, and positive." Then, he blew through the horn while calling out her nickname in his head – *Little Lovie, Little Lovie.*

Fog's expression tightened as if someone were squeezing hate out of his dark, hollow eyes. He looked tortured. Suddenly his grasp on Lady Grace's arm loosened. He released Digger's neck from under his foot as he fell to the floor.

Digger groaned and moved a little. He didn't wake up.

Mrs. Wiggins lay motionless in the corner of the room, covered in frost. As Jackson continued playing the restful, upbeat notes on his horn, the governess slowly regained consciousness.

Everyone kept their eyes on Fastidious Fog out of fear and fascination. As they all watched, Fog began to dissolve from a ghastly, terrifying creature to the grey-haired old man Jackson met at the fair. Twitching and stretching, he changed even more. A younger, distinguished-looking man with greying hair at the temples emerged as he fell into exhaustion and relaxed peace. His soft blue eyes twinkled. Mrs. Wiggins opened her eyes in time to see the entire transformation.

Jackson laughed as he turned to Cherish. "You really are a maker of love."

Cherish touched Jackson gently on the shoulder. "I am the Shaman of Love," she explained. "I am not the *maker* of Love. The only one who *is* Love made me."

What happened next shocked everyone. Fastidious Fog smiled.

Chapter Thirty-Four
Captured

Jackson helped Digger up from the floor as two castle guards came in. They stopped, looked around, and tried to sort out the rescuers from the rescued.

Jackson leaned Jinx against the wall while he got his balance. "Sir, that man, Fastidious Fog, is the Shaman-fey. He terrorized Lady Grace and caused all the ice and crusty frost." Jack looked at Fog, a man transformed. "His Lordship will have to talk to him. Becky and I can give the earl the information we have. It will take someone wiser than I to know what to do with him."

"Thanks," said the guard who entered first. "He'll spend the night in the Lochlan tower. That's where we lock up all those who pose a serious threat to national security." The guard kept his eye on Digger Jinx. "Who is this?"

Mrs. Wiggins shook her head a little. "Mr. Jinx was repairing some thatch on the small tool shed."

"He doesn't look presentable for inside the castle," one guard snapped.

"I was in the kitchen getting a drink of cool water when Lady Grace and Mrs. Wiggins came through. When I started back out to the courtyard, I saw that man, Fog, walk right through the front door. My heart pounded. I knew no one could casually stroll into the castle, so I followed him."

Jackson thought about how Jinx looked. How could the guard take him seriously when Digger dressed like a tramp, a clean tramp, but a tramp all the same. "Mr. Jinx is from Waddyshire," Jackson vouched for Digger. "The Vicar recommended him as an odd-jobber at the castle."

"Thanks, young Jones," Jinx whispered. "I love to watch all the children and make sure they're safe. They remind me of my little angel." Digger's eyes grew sad. "She died with her mummy five years ago, before I moved to Waddyshire."

The guard took Fastidious Fog by the arm to march him out of the nursery. To Jackson and the children, the guard assured them, "You are all safe now." Looking at Dutch as he passed, he added, "Be on guard, pooch."

Dutch responded with a soft, "Woof."

"You need to get back, my Lady," Mrs. Wiggins announced. "I must stay here in the nursery to help Mrs. Kelley. We need to settle the little ones down."

"Rebecca and I can take Lady Grace back to the Cozy Salon. We'll see Mr. Jinx out the door."

"The men guarding the countess will escort Mr. Jinx to the servants' entrance," the other guard assured them.

Mrs. Wiggins and Mrs. Kelley soothed the little ones with words of caring and security. Both governess and nanny held the children on their laps as they rocked them in the large Windsor rocking chairs.

Jackson turned to look for Cherish. His face beamed when he saw the Shaman of Love wave and drift out of the room, like mist lifting on an early morning.

Chapter Thirty-Five

A Surprise

That next week, Broadmoor Castle's ballroom had filled. The earl invited Jackson and all his family, Rebecca and her kin, Uncle Frederick, Aunt Polly, and the cousins. Amazingly, Digger Jinx also received an invitation.

Women from the court were in dresses with full, bell-shaped skirts that swayed and swished when they walked. Bridget made a new dress for herself and one for Jemima. They weren't as fancy as the wealthy women's attire. Still, Bridget felt proud of her needlework when she got dressed that morning in their cottage in Waddyshire.

Jackson saw men wearing name tags with the words, *The Lochlan News.* A newsman placed an easel off to the side of the room.

The ballroom gleamed with gold and white marble that sparkled in the light from the crystal chandeliers. The fragrance of blossoms hung in the air from huge bouquets arranged in crystal vases.

Suddenly, those invited and the many court observers stood up. The Earl of Moorland and Lady Virginia walked in and sat on impressive red velvet chairs. Lady Grace and Lord Thomas came in proudly behind them. They took their places in smaller chairs on the floor level, facing the people. Lady Grace sat regally. Then she smiled and waved two fingers at Jackson, Rebecca, and Jemima.

Jackson smiled as he watched all the people.

All grew silent. The earl began. "I have had a meeting with King Wilber. He agreed that someone deserves to be honored with the King's new order." The earl paused and looked at Lady Virginia. "While the King isn't ready to officially honor his people with the new order, we agree that someone in our midst deserves to be the first one to receive it. We will say he was pre-conferred."

Those watching laughed softly. The grand ladies put a white-gloved hand to their lips. Since no one told those in attendance why their invitation came, excitement hung over the room.

"The King's new honor will be the Royal Victors Order, an order of knighthood. On the King's behalf, I will bestow it on the one I have chosen for his service to the Crown and Country." He paused while a court page brought the knighting sword. "Jackson Jones, will you please come forward?"

Everyone in the Jones family, and their friends with them, gasped in unison. It seemed like a choir conductor had given the signal for the downbeat, and they all inhaled together. Jackson tried not to laugh. He felt his face grow hot. The thought that his cheeks might be bright red embarrassed him. With the golden horn buried in its pouch that hung over his shoulder, he got up slowly, walked toward the front of the room, and bowed.

The earl turned the sword to the flat side of the blade. Then, he lifted the knighting sword and placed the foil on Jackson's right shoulder. "Jackson Jones, you saved the kingdom from life-threatening frost and our precious Lady Grace from death. You saved Broadmoor Castle from freezing, and you saved the Village of Waddyshire, all while playing your horn. You are now a man, taking responsibility for the safety of those around you. You are truly the one. You are the one who can make music to calm the soul. You are the one to dissolve a Shaman's hate. I knight you with the Royal Victors Order for Valor." The earl raised the sword above Jackson's head and flipped it over so the same side of the blade would come to rest on Jackson's left shoulder."

After the ceremony, Jackson approached the earl. He bowed again. "Your Lordship, you need to know something. Yes, like everybody, I'm the one with an important job. But I'm not the one who makes the music. I am the one who holds the horn."

You, too, are the one to hold the horn,

and offer your breath to make the Lord's music.

Recipes

Bread and Butter Pudding

Ingredients:

8 slices of stale bread

½ cup softened butter

½ cup granulated sugar

½ cup dried currants, cranberries, or raisins

1 ¾ cup half and half or milk

2 eggs

1 pinch nutmeg

¼ teaspoon vanilla

Directions:

1. Heat oven to 350°

    Grease a 9-inch cake pan or pie plate

2. Butter the bread on both sides. Cut into triangles. Arrange a single layer of buttered bread in the bottom of the pan, overlapping triangles slightly. Sprinkle with ½ of the sugar and all of the chosen dried fruit. Arrange the remaining triangles of bread, then sprinkle with the remaining sugar.

3. Beat milk, eggs, nutmeg, and vanilla together. Pour over the bread and press firmly to compress the pudding and help it absorb.

4. Bake – 30 minutes - until golden brown

5. Serve with whipped cream, ice cream, or eat on its
    own

Home Made Biscuits

Preheat oven to 450°

Ingredients:

2 cups sifted, all-purpose flour

4 teaspoons baking powder

1 teaspoon salt

4 tablespoons shortening

¾ cup milk

Directions:

Sift flour into a mixing bowl, add baking powder, and salt

Cut shortening into dry ingredients until crumbly.

Add milk and mix just enough to make a soft dough.

Flour breadboard slightly (or clean counter), turn out dough on board, knead a few times gently, and roll gently to ½ to ¾ inch thick.

Cut biscuits with a floured biscuit cutter or knife

Place biscuits onto an ungreased baking sheet.

Bake until lightly browned, about 12 minutes.

Makes 15 to 18 biscuits

Vegetable Stew

2 pounds of stew meat

Vegetables: potatoes, carrots, small onions, and fresh mushrooms (if you like)

1 large can of tomatoes

3 tablespoons tapioca

1 tablespoon salt

Cook in the oven at 300° for 5 hours

Tomato Soup

Ingredients:

2 cups canned tomatoes

1 tablespoon minced onion

2 cups milk

2 tablespoons melted butter

½ Bay leaf

2 tablespoons flour

1 Clove

salt and pepper to taste

Combine the tomatoes with the minced onion, bay leaf, and clove in a pan. Cover. Simmer 10 minutes. Combine butter and flour, add to the tomato puree. Simmer 5 minutes. Add cold milk slowly. Heat to boiling. Season with salt and pepper to taste. Serve at once. Makes 4 servings.

Baked Chicken Chop Suey and Rice

Recipe modified from a chop suey with hamburger

Sauté: In 1 tablespoon butter

one small onion

½ cup celery

In 9x13x2 inch baking dish or pan, mix—

1 cup rice (minute)

1 can cream of mushroom soup undiluted

1 can cream chicken soup, undiluted

3 ½ cups boiling water

5 tablespoons soy sauce

1 tablespoon brown sugar

Place chicken tenders, cut in half, over the top

Bake at 350° for 45 minutes

Last 15 minutes, top all with 1 can Fancy Chow Mein Noodles

About the Author
Doris Gaines Rapp, Ph.D.

Doris Gaines Rapp, Ph.D., author, psychologist, educator, and speaker, has written over a dozen novels and several non-fiction books. Her books are loved by all those who read them. Doris enjoys painting and drawing, including the covers of three of her books and the interior pages of one. She has sung for many groups and has written songs she shares with others. Readers continue to ask for additional books in her series, *Tucker McBride*. They love the characters, the history, and the tales of adventure and antics. While still a full-time psychologist, Doris directed the counseling centers at Taylor University and then Bethel University. She has taught undergraduate and graduate courses in psychology at local universities. Twenty years after she and her husband raised their first family, they adopted two little girls. Now that all six children have filled the world around them, the Rapps enjoy their small-town life. Doris loves the stories that burst forth from her computer, and Bill still serves as a pastor and Chaplin. Her desire for all of you — "I hope you live all of your life."

Other Novels by Doris Gaines Rapp, Ph.D.

Fiction

Tucker's Perfect Day	2021
Tucker McBride's Many Lives	2020
Tucker McBride	2019
News at Eleven - A Novel	2015
Just in Time - Murder, She Blogged	2020
Length of Days Trilogy	2020
Shyloe and the Mayor	2018
Escape from the Belfry: Second Edition	2017
Escape from the Shadows	2017
Length of Days - Search for Freedom	2016
Length of Days - Beyond the Valley of the Keepers	2015
Length of Days - The Age of Silence	2014
Hiawassee - Child of the Meadow	2014
Smoke from Distant Fires	2014

Non-Fiction

Pray Them to Heaven	2021
Prayer for Release from Anxiety	2015
Prayer Therapy of Jesus	2014
Christmases Past Anne Baxter Campbell, Andrea Merrell, Doris Rapp, et al.	2014
Waiting for Jesus in a Can't Wait World: Advent	2014
Promote Yourself	2013
Holding on to Sand - From the Interactive Journal of James Rapp	2012